Chrysalis

Angie Martin

Happy Reading!
♡ A

This edition published by Angie Martin for CreateSpace
Text © Angie Martin 2017
ISBN-13: 978-1984132710
ISBN-10: 1984132717

Cover Art by: Amanda Walker
Edited by: CJ Pinard

To learn more about author Angie Martin,
please visit her website at www.angiemartinbooks.com

This work of fiction contains adult situations that may not be suitable for children under eighteen years of age. Recommended for mature audiences only.

Novels by Angie Martin

Rachel Thomas Novels
False Security (Book 1)
False Hope (Book 2)

Emily Monroe Novels
Conduit

Standalone Novels
The Boys Club

Poetry / Short Story collections
Shadows
the three o'clock in the morning sessions

Anthologies
Eye of Fear
The Cat, the Crow, and the Cauldron
Discovery

Dedication

For Marisa. You keep inspiring me every day.

Prologue

The gray is a test from God.

Peter Holbrook repeated his mother's mantra over and over, hopeful that the impending gloom of the afternoon's rainfall would disappear into a rainbow of hope cascading over his immature mind. The "gray" they called the Spring storms in his small town of Nowhere, Kansas, and it seemed to take over the souls of everyone living in the area during its annual visit. It was especially trying for a teenager in the hospital.

Though two years had passed since his last trip to the hospital, Peter swore it looked and smelled the same, as if residing in the middle of a time warp, refusing to acknowledge the progress of the rest of the world. As much as he did two years earlier, Peter hated the stench, a putrid mix of bleach and illness with a hint of death.

His warm breath fogged the window, and he swirled his fingertip in a nondescript pattern. Something to help draw him out of the slight depression that always came with the gray and his extended hospital stays.

As if an answer direct from heaven to cheer him, a kaleidoscope of butterflies swarmed on the horizon, flying closer to him with each flap of their tiny wings. He grazed the chilled window with his fingers, wiping away the sweat from the inside of the glass, just enough so he could sneak a better glimpse of nature's finest.

One butterfly broke away from the group and came up to the window. Peter's forehead touched the glass as he stared into its eyes. It remained in front of him, relaying some kind of secret message, though Peter could not guess what it attempted to say. For all its inability to speak, it mesmerized him with flashes of color in its wings. Blues, greens, oranges, even reds… so many colors that Peter had never seen in one creature. Then, as if realizing it was getting nowhere with him in communication, it flew away and rejoined its friends.

Turning his attention away from the foggy, age-stained window, he shuffled back to his bed, one hand holding the back of his hospital gown closed, the other dragging an IV pole behind him. He eased himself into bed. Once somewhat comfortable, his left hand blindly searched the bed for the remote, an ingrained response to his surroundings. He had no intention of watching television. An exploration of the channels in the middle of a Thursday afternoon would only bring up soap operas and talk shows. Though Days of Our Lives had recently become his guilty pleasure and his mother had made Phil Donohue a staple in their home, at the moment, neither of them appeased the mind of thirteen-year-old Peter.

Instead, he gazed at the window. Not outside the window, but at the window itself. Looking beyond that, at the gray, would give him nothing but heartache, especially since his mid-afternoon entertainment had flown away.

The gray is a test from God.

According to his well-meaning mother, everything was a test from God, a blessing he only needed to decipher. Everything from the gloomy, yearly rains clouding his hometown to the epilepsy that sometimes clenched his brain and controlled him… all God's tests. The epilepsy used to frighten Peter, until his mother explained it was only a hug from angels. They loved him so much they often became overly excited to see him, encircling him in a fierce grip and jumping up and down with him, not realizing the repercussions on his young, non-ethereal brain.

Though Peter knew angels did not hug him when a seizure came, he embraced the explanation and loved his mother even more for it. The comfort she provided him through her faith was enough to make him believe himself. God and angels and apostles and all that followed.

Then came the belief that Peter himself was destined for something good. Something pure. Something more than the typical life promised to a small-town boy growing up in the Midwest. His mother acted more as prophetess for Peter than a Bible-thumping, over-reacting, end-of-the-world spouting religious freak – the kind who preached that all things worldly were sinful and used by the Devil to lure the unsuspecting into his hypnotic trail of death and flames. No, Peter's mother was love: the love of the Word, the love of God, the love of Jesus. A bright light who shone on Peter and all who crossed her path. And, everyone loved her in return.

Peter's mother made him *believe*. Believe in more than creek beds and sewer snakes, believe in more than hunting bucks and fingernails dirty with boyhood. Peter believed in God.

But, along with that came the Devil and the demons. Forces of evil that craved destruction.

The gray may be a test from God, Peter conceded, but the gray housed the demons.

And, the demons terrified him.

Chapter One

Eighteen years later…

Bitter coffee swished through Sheriff Peter Holbrook's mouth, waking him up in the worst of ways. He reached for the glass sugar dispenser and lifted it above his mug. White crystals flooded through the small, metal hole in the top of the container, racing for their turn to dissolve in the hot liquid.

Sampling the coffee, Peter deemed it the perfect mix of sugar with the hot brew and set his mug down on the white with silver trim 50s diner counter. The smell of bacon grease penetrated every plastic-covered red and white booth and stool, as if the diner only offered that one item on its menu. An institution in Nowhere, the diner was part of a long-past, frozen era, the same as the rest of the town.

Peter folded his hands and enjoyed the banter from the local residents, who also frequented the diner every morning. Gossip floated through the air in tones just above a whisper, as if the speakers wished everyone to know they had heard about the latest small-town controversy first.

Interrupting his eavesdropping on the townsfolk, Hannah O'Brien shoved Peter's tan-colored sheriff's hat across the counter to his right side, and then slid a plate with a single slice of buttered white toast in front of him. He raised his gaze just in time to catch one of her olive-green eyes winking at him as she walked away. The corners of his mouth turned upward, and he reached for grape jelly packets. As soon as she left, his fingertips combed through his dirty-blond hair, making it obey for long enough so Hannah wouldn't find him slovenly. He thanked God he remembered to shave that morning. She always gave him grief about too many days' growth on his jaw.

Hannah had inherited the diner from her ailing father two years ago, and Peter looked forward to seeing her every morning at breakfast and some evenings at dinner. His first love from the days when they had shared their Legos and Tinker Toys, Hannah always held a special place in his heart. Having grown up together, first in Wichita, then moving to Nowhere when their fathers were both laid off from Cessna, Hannah knew Peter better than anyone, yet they did nothing about their mutual, suppressed feelings. Their timelines and stars never matched up quite right for either of them to make the leap.

When Peter had finally worked himself up to ask her out, she ran off to college and moved in with some guy. After that didn't take and she returned to Nowhere, Peter had his sights on a girl from Andover, though it only lasted six months. In the years since, they both avoided the topic of a possible relationship. Still, Hannah remained flirty, and Peter pulled her pigtails every so often. Maybe, one day, the hints would evolve into something more, which he would welcome. Until then, their unspoken arrangement suited Peter just fine.

A friendly bump jolted Peter's arm as he sipped his coffee, which he almost spilled. He craned his head around to glance over his shoulder.

"Sorry, Sher'ff," Fred McAllister said. "I weren't watchin' too good."

Peter cracked a smile. "No harm done, Fred. How's Belinda feeling this morning?"

Fred bellied up next to Peter and plopped his bony elbows onto the counter. His dark, bushy eyebrows, ones that belonged on a man three times the age of Fred's thirty-four years, cinched together. "Good, good, but cranky as a chicken with a stuck egg. I figure another week, and we'll have our new lil 'un. If we don't, I might have to take 'er out to the shop to see if we can get 'er out of there. I can't take Belinda's fussin' much more."

"Let your wife complain," Peter said. "She's bringing your child into the world."

"That's enough to make any woman scream and complain," Hannah said from behind the counter. She set a clean ceramic mug down in front of Fred, and coffee rained down from a decanter she held over it. She fiddled with the blue pen behind her ear and asked, "The usual for ya, Fred?"

"S'long as Maureen ain't making dem fancy eggs back there, the usual is fine."

She flipped her wavy, auburn hair behind her shoulder and pursed her full, glossy lips. "We still only serve two kinds of eggs here: scrambled and fried."

"Gimme scrambled and cook 'em well. Ain't good for you to eat stuff raw that God meant to be cooked. He din't give us fire for nuthin'."

Peter chuckled under his breath and gulped his sugary coffee. Fred and Hannah had engaged in the same conversation every morning for as long as Peter could remember, and they would continue to have it until the end of their days. He relished that about his simple life. Predictable, reliable. Perfect.

Hannah's hips unintentionally swished inside her form-fitting jeans as she sauntered back to give the order to Maureen, the diner's long-time cook. Peter stared a moment too long, looking away right before Hannah turned around.

"Got a busy day 'head ya?" Fred asked him.

Though Peter didn't mind the conversation, he'd rather sit silently and daydream about Hannah before his day began. "Nothing out of the ordinary."

"Really? You're not goin' to da clinic?" Fred asked.

"Why would I go there?"

"The girl. I thought you'd be down thar already, but then I seen you here."

Peter's eyes floated to the side, and his brow raised. "What girl are you talking about?"

"The girl that wrecked this mornin'."

Setting down his coffee mug, Peter swiveled on his stool. "What wreck, Fred?"

"The one that dun happened outside limits. O'er on the east side, off of ol' 54."

"Sounds like I'd be at the clinic if someone had bothered to tell me," Peter said, a tinge of annoyance clipping his words. "I keep telling y'all, if you don't call Shirley and tell her what's happened, I won't know. And, if I don't know, I can't help. Can't rely on gossip to solve crime and keep this town under control."

"Well, don't get your britches bunched up," Fred said. "I thought someone else called Shirley, but they musta thought someone else did, too. Mixed in the crosshairs, I s'pose."

"I'm sure that's what happened. Was there another vehicle involved?"

"Unh-uh. Just the girl and her Ford. Hugged a tree with her passenger side, but no tellin' how she got thar. From the damage, looks like she drove the limit. At least she was drivin' 'merican. That's what prolly saved her, that sturdy Ford. Dem overseas cars ain't worth a damn thang."

Peter rose from his stool and retrieved his wallet from his back pocket. Glaring at his unfinished slice of jelly toast, he threw down a five-dollar bill for his $1.85 breakfast plus tip, the same amount he did every day. "These roads get a little slick when the gray comes," he said, referring to the spring storms that plagued their area every year. "Especially at night. I'm sure she swerved to miss colliding with a critter and couldn't keep control. Is the car already at your shop to get fixed?"

"Sure is," Fred said. "Towed it over thar an hour ago."

"Next time there's a wreck, let's leave the car in place until I can see it."

"Will do, Sher'ff."

Peter slapped his hat on his head and raised his hand in Hannah's direction, receiving an overly friendly smile in return. Moving toward the front door, nodding at some patrons he passed, he considered where to go first. He settled on the clinic to check on the girl and get her statement. Then, he would head to Fred's shop to look at the car. Finally, he'd backtrack to the site of the wreck to make sure it and the damage to the car corroborated her story. A full day scheduled before eight in the morning. He couldn't remember the last time that happened in his sleepy town.

He opened the diner door, turned right, toward his patrol car, and stopped. Butterflies of all sizes and colors lined the roof of his car, as if they conspired to lift it into the air and carry it away. Peter blinked at the sight, and slowly, the butterflies left his car, one by one. They drifted into the spring morning, lighting up the gray like the tail of a colorful kite, their movements purposeful, as if they wanted Peter to watch their dance.

His feet glided to his car, propelled by the same mysterious force controlling the butterflies. At the driver's side door, a single

ANGIE MARTIN

butterfly remained. A strange pattern in the yellows and oranges seared Peter's retinas and paralyzed him. Only one other butterfly had ever caught his attention like this one, but he had been a teenager in the hospital. Surely, he had dreamt that other encounter, but he wasn't imagining this one.

The butterfly lifted off the white paint of his car, kissed Peter's nose, and followed its group. The spell broken, Peter opened his door and started the car. He drove off toward the butterflies, toward the clinic.

Chapter Two

The tires of Peter's patrol car sloshed through puddles, sending rainwater flying out in all directions as he drove toward the clinic that served the 382 residents of Nowhere, Kansas. He glanced at the speedometer and told himself to slow down, but his foot didn't listen. It stayed firmly pressed on the accelerator with the exact amount of force to keep his speed at thirty-five miles per hour, ten over the legal limit on Main Street, and about fifteen over for the wet road conditions.

Peter never used his sheriff status to drive over the limit, unless his lights swirled red and blue and sirens sang through the streets, but the butterflies stuck in his mind. Focused on the phenomenon, he cared little about breaking traffic laws. The touch of the butterfly lingered on his nose. A strange occurrence on its own, but with the rest of the butterflies on the roof of his vehicle, he didn't know what to make of it. Combined with a girl crashing her car on the outskirts of town, his whole morning had shifted into the realm of bizarre. Much more so than anything he'd handled during his tenure as sheriff.

The job of sheriff landed in Peter's lap ten years earlier, though he had never intended for his career as a deputy to go so far. The reigning sheriff, Roger Schlitz, had suffered a massive heart attack during a routine traffic stop. In the hospital, he declared his 43-year stint over, leaving Nowhere County without a leading lawman. All eyes had instantly turned to Peter, the senior deputy at the time, despite having only three years on the job. As long as he kept the town running, and the dognappings and bar brawls to a minimum, he'd have no trouble serving as sheriff for the rest of his working years.

His patrol car turned onto Vine Avenue, twenty minutes west of the diner. As he steered into the parking lot of the clinic, Peter mused that the accident victim must not be too bad off if she had not been transferred to a larger hospital in Wichita. He had exhausted his theories on how she ended up in a one-car wreck so early in the morning, but he'd learn the story soon enough.

As soon as he ambled through the automatic doors into the clinic, Deputy Oliver Esparza waved Peter over to his position against the wall in the lobby. "Hey, Sheriff."

"How'd you get here so soon, Ollie?"

"Shirley called."

The news did not surprise Peter, but he still asked, "She called you, but not me?"

"She said she heard you were already on your way. I was a block over and thought you might want some help."

Peter shook his head at the inefficient way his office handled calls. He had tried to resolve it over the years, but a small-town sheriff's office with a stubborn gal like Shirley had its ways fixed. "Do you have anything else going on this morning?" he asked.

"Just another property line dispute over at the Whitaker farm. I figured I'd come out here to help you and then head out that way."

"What's the disagreement today?"

"The usual. Wyatt Whitaker says Keith Dusky had his plane drop pesticides on his crops yesterday."

The Whitaker/Dusky border war had been ongoing for years. If it wasn't Keith's pesticides, it was Wyatt's cattle or dogs wandering across the border. "What's Keith's story?" Peter asked.

"He says his plane has to fly over Wyatt's crop. It's the flight plan. He also says nothing was unloaded until it got over his own crop."

"All right, I've had enough of this damn dispute," Peter said. "Tell them that if they can't straighten this out and call us again, they'll be fined for misuse of the 911 system."

"They didn't call 911. They called Shirley."

"Then, it's misuse of the Shirley system. Order them to get a surveyor out here to settle the matter and they can pony-up half each for the cost. I want it done by month's end."

"You got it, Sheriff."

Peter leaned against the wall and jerked his head toward the double doors leading to the patient rooms. "What's the story with our girl this morning?"

"Been waiting for you to get here so we can go see her. Lou Ann says she's awake and alert, but not talking much. Also, she thinks the girl is from Los Angeles or New York or something."

"Driver's license say that?"

"Nah," Ollie said. "Girl's covered in tattoos. Like from up here," he held his hand out flat under his chin, "all the way down to her toes. Even her hands, Lou Ann says."

Peter frowned. "Just 'cause the girl has some ink doesn't mean she's from a big city. Lots of people getting tattoos these days."

Ollie's shoulders lifted. "Maybe she's a tattoo artist? They usually have a lot of 'em."

"Maybe."

Lou Ann, the head nurse in the clinic, emerged through the doors. Peter and Ollie both straightened themselves out and started toward her.

"Sheriff, Ollie," Lou Ann said, patting her gray hair pulled back in her usual tidy bun. "Glad you two are here."

"How's your patient, Lou Ann?" Peter asked.

"Poor girl's been through the ringer. Mostly superficial cuts and bruises, but she hit her head pretty hard on the steering wheel. 'Fraid she has a bit of amnesia."

Peter tilted his head. "Amnesia?"

"You'll have to ask Doc Horton more about it. He's in there with her now." She gestured for them to follow her through the doors to the rooms where they kept overnight and short-term patients.

Behind her, Peter and Ollie exchanged a curious look. A single car wreck in the early morning, a woman covered in tattoos, and now she had amnesia. Peter's morning was becoming more interesting by the second.

They continued down the hall, two steps behind Lou Ann, until they reached room 112. It was the largest single-patient room on the floor. Peter assumed they had precious few other guests for them to offer it to this girl, a stranger to their town.

Lou Ann eased the door open and led them into the room. Jeffrey Horton, the town doctor, glanced up at them, his mouth curving into a smile. He shook both men's hands and returned to his chart.

Peter peeked at the patient, who shifted in her bed when she caught his eyes. He moved to the wall and pulled a chair over to the bed, facing her. Sitting down to make her more comfortable and doing his best not to stare at the black ink on her neck and arms, he smiled. "Welcome to Nowhere," he said. "Glad to have you, just not in these circumstances."

Her eyes widened, and Peter jolted back, the hundred questions he had for her stuck in his throat. Her left eye shone bluer than any he'd ever seen. Her right one, though, matched the midnight sky in the country, the color of the iris so deep that it almost matched her pupil. With her stick-straight shoulder-blade length hair the color of Hannah's coffee and her black tattoos standing out against pale skin, Peter was sure he'd remember her appearance for the rest of his life.

Doc Horton walked to the opposite side of the bed and rescued Peter from his eternal silence. "Our patient has had quite an accident. She arrived here around four this morning. Dan Wheaton brought her in and called me on his way. He said her engine was cold, so she had to have been there for a while, unconscious. She has contusions on her legs, chest, and face, all consistent with an auto accident. A few lacerations, but nothing needing stitches, so she's lucky in that regard. She checks out physically, but has very little memory."

"Does she remember her name?" Ollie asked.

"Kaylen," a timid voice said from the bed.

Peter turned to her once more to find her staring at him.

"My name is Kaylen, but that's all I remember."

Peter offered what he hoped was a reassuring smile. "It's okay, Kaylen. We'll get the rest figured out." Looking back at Doc Horton, he said, "Tell us about the amnesia."

"Appears to be retrograde, meaning she remembers nothing before the accident. Her MRI showed some minor swelling on the brain, but everything else, including bloodwork, came back normal. She remembered her name about an hour ago, but nothing else has come back so far. She has complete motor function and knows how to perform tasks, at least the ones we tested her on."

"Purse, ID?" Peter asked. "Anything at the scene or in the car? Registration and insurance card in the glovebox?"

"Nothing was found that we know of," Ollie said. "I called over to Fred's repair shop and had Dustin search the car."

"She had no purse when she came in, and no wallet in her jeans," Lou Ann said.

Peter fixed his eyes back on Kaylen. "Ma'am, do you mind if I search your jeans?"

She shook her head. "Go right ahead. I'd love some answers."

Lou Ann opened the closet door and pulled out the woman's blue jeans. Nothing stood out to Peter about the denim clothing. He checked each pocket and came up empty. Handing them back to Lou Ann, he said, "Well, looks like we have a bit of a mystery here. Do you mind if I grab a picture of you to start our investigation?"

Kaylen squirmed, but agreed with a nod.

Peter retrieved his cell phone from his pocket and snapped a photo of her face. He lowered his phone a bit to get her neck tattoos in the frame, but his camera didn't flash. Assuming his phone's memory was full, he slipped his phone back in his pocket and asked, "Doc, when will she be ready for discharge?"

"I want to keep her overnight for observation, make sure there are no other issues. Probably release her around nine tomorrow morning, if that works?"

"I… I don't know where I'd go," Kaylen said, the sadness in her voice conflicting with concern.

"Don't you worry at all," Peter said. "We won't let you go without a plan. I'll make sure you're well taken care of until you have a home to go to."

Kaylen's exhale was all the gratitude Peter needed. Rising from his chair, he patted the bed rail. "You just rest today. I'll be back around tomorrow. Until then, stay out of trouble." He winked at her warm smile.

Ollie fell in step next to Peter as soon as they left the room. "What do you need from me?" he asked.

The frown returned to Peter's face. "Call Delores at the inn and see if she can get a room ready for Kaylen so she has a place to stay tomorrow night. I'm gonna head over to Fred's shop and then to where she wrecked."

"Works for me," Ollie said. "I'll call Delores on the way to the Dusky property."

"Tell her charge me for the room until we figure this out."

"You sure?"

"Least we can do for the girl," Peter said. "She may have a long road ahead of her in this memory thing."

"Do you want Shirley to get photos of her out to Wichita and the other towns?"

Peter started to answer in the affirmative, but a knot formed in his stomach. "Not yet, Ollie. Let's make sure she's okay to be released from the hospital and give her a night to see if her memory returns. But, have Shirley gather recent missing persons reports from the area. We may get lucky that way."

The automatic doors to the outside opened, and they stepped into the thick of the gray. Fog had encased the clinic in the short time they had been inside.

"Damn this weather," Ollie muttered.

"Once a year," Peter said. "We only have to do this once a year."

"Thank God, or else I'd leave for good. It'd be worse than Seattle."

"What do you know about Seattle?" Peter asked, smirking. He knew Ollie had barely left the state, and that was to go to Oklahoma City for a law enforcement conference a couple years earlier.

"I know enough to know I don't wanna live there," Ollie said. He waved and jogged toward his patrol car.

Peter chuckled to himself and headed for his own car as rain sputtered to the ground around him. "Great," he said. Maybe it was worse in Nowhere than in Seattle.

With his full day looming ahead, he climbed into his car and glanced at his watch out of habit. He shoved his keys in the ignition, but paused before starting the engine. The tattoos on the woman stood out in his mind, as if he should recognize them. As he rolled them around in his thoughts, he realized they weren't pictures, as he originally believed, but symbols of some sort.

He leaned back in his seat and stared at the clinic. No butterflies. Contrary to all logic, he had expected to see them swarming the building. He stared for a long moment, waiting for one to appear. While he watched, one of the tattooed symbols floated in his mind's eye.

A crack of thunder broke him out of his hypnotic state. Starting the engine, the clock on his stereo caught his attention. Over an hour had passed since he first shut his car door. He took a second look at his watch to make sure the time was right. It matched his car clock.

"That's impossible," he said. There was no explanation for a few seconds lapsing into more than an hour, but it had happened. As he put the car into drive, he decided to keep the incident to himself.

Chapter Three

The eyesore known as McAllister Auto and Salvage functioned as the only auto and farm equipment repair shop in an over 40-mile radius. Fred grew up in the shop, often inviting childhood friends like Peter over to run amok through the acres of hollow shells of long-deceased vehicles, a strange form of skeletal survival, left clinging to the ground like cicadas to trees.

Walking up the side drive to the office, the ubiquitous rust and thick scent of motor oil reminded Peter of those days and the many tetanus shots his mother forced upon him due to random cuts and scrapes on questionable hunks of metal. He subconsciously rubbed his upper left arm, as if stuck by a phantom needle, and stopped at the door to the office. The sign was flipped to CLOSED, but when he pressed his forehead against the glass, he couldn't spot much past the thick layers of grime. Belinda, Fred's wife, used to clean the office, but her last two months of pregnancy had worn her thin and left her on bed rest. Peter supposed once the baby came, the cleaning would resume.

Despite the sign, he twisted the doorknob, but the lock resisted. He shuffled on behind the office, where bays housed vehicles for repair. It wasn't unusual for Fred to lock up the shop while working on a job.

He spied Fred pacing outside the back entrance to the bays, a cigarette mashed between his lips. A puff of smoke escaped his nostrils, and Peter grinned. As soon as Fred turned his back, Peter crept up behind him, keeping his footfalls light so as not to give away his position.

When he was only a few steps away from Fred, he asked,

"Whatcha doin' there?"

A cough preceded Fred whirling around. The cigarette flew from his fingertips and into a patch of damp, spring grass, one of the few on the premises.

Peter shook his head and went to the cigarette. He picked it up, holding it as if it would explode at any second, and took it back to Fred. "You're not really going to litter in front of me, are you? A lit cigarette, no less?"

"Don't tell Belinda," Fred said, snatching the cigarette from Peter's fingers. "I don't need no grief from her."

"I thought you quit for the baby."

"And, I'll quit again when she decides to get 'ere. I think the lil' bugger's coming today. My bones just know it."

"Your bones are rarely wrong."

"Hey, you can't tell Belinda, ya hear me? I ne'er told your daddy about that joint you snuck back in high school."

"And, I never told your pa that you stole a few drags off it, either."

Fred gazed past Peter, drifting somewhere into the past, a whimsical smile crossing the graying stubble on his jaw. "That was one of the best days."

"Did absolutely nothing for me."

Fred glanced at him and shrugged. "Ya did it wrong."

Both men gave into hearty laughter at their shared joke from years past. They would never know if Peter smoked pot incorrectly the first and only time he tried it, but the experience always made them chuckle as if they were still high.

After their laughing died down, Peter asked, "You got a car for me to look at?"

Fred gestured for Peter to follow him into the vehicle bays. "Number five, second from the end." He slowed until he walked side-by-side with Peter. As if they were in a crowd full of eavesdroppers, he whispered. "Is it true the girl's all tattooed?"

Peter knew that one detail wouldn't take long to make it around town. Instead of answering the question, he asked, "What's wrong with some tattoos? You have a few yourself."

"Dem Army tats. Don't count." Before Peter could fully process the statement, Fred said, "Thar she is."

Other than the mud that had sprayed the driver's side door and the deployed airbag, the white Ford Taurus didn't appear to have been in an accident. He carefully walked around the front of the car, inspecting everything he could. The passenger's side told a different story, with the door smashed inward. The window had shattered, presumably on impact. Gazing into the car, Peter took note of glass on the driver's seat, which explained Kaylen's cuts. Peter was surprised she didn't have a few broken bones to go along with the amnesia. Had there been a passenger in the car, the tree would have blown them the kiss of death.

"Bad, huh?"

Peter shook his head. "Worse than what I thought. What the hell caused her to crash?"

Though the question was rhetorical in nature, Fred said, "I think she weren't alone on the road."

"What do you mean?" he asked, following Fred to the back of the car.

"I didn't see 'em dis morning, but thar's scratches back 'ere. Small dent, too."

Peter leaned over, and he peered at where Fred's fingers pointed at the driver's side, near the brake light. "I'll be damned," he said, running his fingers over a few flecks of red paint embedded in the dent. "Someone hit her."

"If they'd been goin' too fast, it would be worse. They clipped her, and she prolly spun out."

"Stopping when she hit the tree." Peter rose to his full height. "I pray it's not one of our folk who did this."

"I'll scrape that paint for ya. Maybe help ya find the car."

Peter nodded, the thought having already run through his mind when he saw the foreign paint. "I'll send someone down to get pictures first and have a crime scene tech from Wichita come to scrape the paint. Not that I don't trust you," he added to not hurt Fred's feelings, "but if we have to prosecute someone for the hit-and-run, we need it done by the book. In the meantime, can you get me a list of your buddies in the shops around here? Say, within a couple hours' drive? I want to give them a call to look out for a red vehicle with front-end damage."

"Sure thang, Sher'ff."

"One more thing. Could someone have done this on purpose?" Peter hated to think that way, but he had to look at the accident from every possible angle.

"Course, but no way to tell from dis. Maybe someone tried to pass and—" Fred's cell phone rang, and he yanked it out of his back pocket. "Belinda callin'."

"Take your time," Peter said. He walked back around the car, his concern for Kaylen growing. If someone had deliberately tried to run her off the road, they intended to kill her. She could be in trouble. Even if it were an accident, the suspect fled the scene, and probably for some nefarious reason. None of his townsfolk came to mind as someone capable of leaving her to die. Anyone could do anything, he reminded himself, but he hadn't met someone that cold-hearted in his whole life. He certainly didn't want to now.

Fred came charging back to the car. "She's in labor!" he yelled between shallow, jagged breaths. "Oh, my dear Lord above in Heaven, what am I gon' do?"

Peter chuckled. "You're gonna go to the hospital."

"She's havin' the baby down at the clinic. Doc Horton has someone comin' in for it."

"Where's Belinda at now?"

"Her mama's trailer. Thar on the way to the doc."

"Then you better get down there, fast. But, first, Fred? Go spray some cologne, wash your hands, and brush your teeth."

Fred looked at him, confusion crossing his vacant eyes, all thoughts apparently lost with Belinda's call.

"The cigarette?" Peter reminded him.

Fred's eyes widened. "I dun fergot!"

"It's okay," Peter said, slapping him on the upper arm. "Just calm down and get over there. Do you want me to drive you?'

"No, no, Sher'ff. I got it. Thank ya."

Peter watched him barrel out of the bays, unable to wipe the smile off his lips. A new baby. Just the thing the McAllisters needed. Fred would make a wonderful father, and when he stumbled, Belinda would be there to pick him up. The town could use a new youngin, too. That child would be loved by all, and Fred and Belinda would never run out of free babysitters.

He turned his attention back to Kaylen's car. There were no rental stickers on it, so he surmised it was her car. He jotted down the Kansas license plate number, making note of the Sedgwick County sticker on the plate. He'd have Shirley call the plates into the DMV and see if Kaylen came from Wichita or a nearby town. Maybe it would bring them some more information.

After popping the trunk, he inspected the space, only to find nothing other than a spare tire and standard jack under the mat. Nothing in the glove compartment, no purse, wallet, ID, or anything to identify the girl.

As he walked over to the passenger's side to survey the damage once more, his stomach sank. Kaylen could have easily died that morning, especially if she weren't wearing a seatbelt. Yet, because of the safety equipment and the sturdy Ford, as Fred said, Kaylen survived.

He left the bays and headed toward his car. Just as he opened his door, his radio sounded, but it only crackled unintelligible words. Depressing the button on the side of the radio, he leaned his head in its direction and said, "Come again?"

"Sheriff... need... fast..."

"Ollie, is that you?"

"Keith's farm... can't... shotgun..."

Peter jumped in his car and started the engine. "I'm on my way."

Only more static came from the radio. Peter turned onto the main street, his sirens blaring as he listened intently for anything more from his deputy.

Finally, Ollie's voice came back through the radio. "No!" he yelled, followed by a gunshot.

Chapter Four

E yes focused on his path, knuckles turning white from his tense hold on the steering wheel, the gunshot echoed in Peter's ears, pushing him faster to his destination. He navigated the slick back roads to the Whitaker farm a little too fast, his tires sliding on the mud from the morning's rain, but managed to keep his car out of the ditch.

After the shot, he had radioed a distressed Shirley, who had also heard the gunfire, and ordered every available deputy to the scene, along with an ambulance from the clinic. He hated to think of someone on the receiving end of the shotgun's blast, but he had to be prepared for anything.

As he rounded the corner onto the main road that both farms shared, he caught sight of Ollie's patrol car, behind which Ollie stood, gun out and pointed at a screaming, red-faced Keith Dusky. Wyatt Whitaker cowered behind Ollie, something anyone would do when faced with an angry and armed enemy. A quick once-over of all three parties brought instant relief to Peter's mind; no blood, no gaping holes from a shotgun shell.

Peter unlatched his holster and readied his gun as he approached the men on foot. "Keith," he said cautiously to grab the man's attention. "Why don't you put the shotgun down? We can work everything out without the weapon."

"I don't think so, Sheriff," Keith called out, then turned his eyes back to Wyatt. "I'm tired of this two-bit, no good, lyin', stealin' arrogant, son of a—"

"Don't you bring my mama into this!" Wyatt shouted from behind Ollie. "Your mama was the one sleepin' with e'ry trucker that passed through town!"

"Wyatt!" Peter warned. "Stop antagonizing him."

"No, Sheriff," Keith said in an eerily calm tone. "My mama was a whore. My daddy could be one of a million guys that rolled into town that summer she got knocked up. Could be the same guy that gave her that bout of chlamydia, but we'll never know now that she's dead."

Peter's jaw fell open. Sure, he'd heard rumors about Linda Dusky, but Keith had never once failed to defend his mama's honor.

Keith lowered the gun as a laugh escaped him. "Now, she's whoring around hell with the devil as her pimp." His eyes brightened as if he'd just told a prize-winning joke at the county fair. When he doubled over with laughter, the gun hit the ground. His arms wrapped around his rotund belly as he lost himself in a case of the giggles, something Peter hadn't seen out of a grown man, but from boy-crazy teenage girls.

Peter nodded to Ollie, who kept his gun trained on Keith. Peter ran over and snatched up the shotgun from the ground.

Ollie came up to them and pulled out his handcuffs just as two patrol cars parked behind the scene. "Keith Dusky," Ollie said, "you're under arrest for attempted murder, unlawful discharge of a firearm…"

Ollie continued with the charges and reading of the Miranda warning as he handcuffed Keith, but Peter tuned him out when the words "attempted murder" sent his thoughts into a tailspin. Connecting that crime to anyone in his town, let alone Keith Dusky, was as insane as Keith's ramblings.

He looked up to see Ollie standing in front of him with the prisoner.

Deputies Doug Shultz and Len Carter raced up to them. "No one's hurt?" Doug asked. "I heard a shot."

"We're good," Ollie said. "He fired into the air."

"I'll take Keith in with Ollie," Peter said. The lights and sirens of the incoming ambulance caught his attention. "Len and Doug, get Wyatt's statement and have the paramedics look him over just to be safe."

"Gotcha, Sheriff," Len said.

"Crazy morning, ain't it?" Ollie asked as he walked with Peter to the patrol car.

"Hoping this is the end of it," Peter said.

Next to him, Keith broke out in giggles again… high-pitched and crazed, like nothing Peter had ever heard.

"Stay here a second," Peter told Ollie. He guided a hysterical Keith into the back of his patrol car. "Just sit still," he said, slamming the door shut. Walking back to Ollie, he shook his head and tried to wrap his brain around what just happened.

"What the hell is wrong with Keith?" Ollie asked.

"We'll have Shirley call Doc Horton. I want him to come down to the station to assess Keith's physical health. Make sure he hasn't been exposed to something that's warped his brain."

"Don't want him going in the ambulance straight to the clinic?"

"I'd rather have him in jail, keep everyone safe."

Ollie snorted. "May have to get a shrink down here as well."

"Let's have Doc Horton take his turn first, then he can bring someone else out as he sees fit." He started to walk away, but remembered Kaylen and his discovery at Fred's shop. "When he's done here, send Doug out to the accident site to make sure no one disturbs it until I get out there."

"Something the matter?"

"Looks like someone else hit her and caused the accident." Another thought struck him, one he might have already had if Keith hadn't lost his mind. "Will you radio in Chuck to sit on her room for the rest of the day? If this was an intentional act, then whoever did it might come after her."

Ollie's eyebrows reached for his mass of slicked-back, black hair. "This day is pretty damn exciting, and not in a good way."

"Definitely not," Peter said, climbing into his patrol car. "Meet ya down there."

He slid into the driver's seat, relieved Keith had fallen silent. Once he steered the car onto the main road leading to the sheriff's station, he glanced in the rearview mirror at his now-subdued passenger. Keith stared out the window, a blank expression on his face, almost as if in a trance of sorts. Saliva dribbled from the corner of his mouth, rolled down the side of his chin, and slowly dripped in thick drops somewhere on Keith's clothes. Before Peter could say anything, Keith wiped his mouth with the shoulder of his dusty flannel shirt. The spittle smeared across his skin, painting it with a glistening layer of brownish fluid.

Peter could no longer keep his thoughts locked away. "Keith, what happened today? Is there something you want to tell me about?"

Keith didn't acknowledge the questions, not with a nod, a quick look, a grunt, groan, or anything suggesting he was still alive to hear and comprehend them.

"Look," Peter said, "I know Ollie read you your rights, and you're under no obligation to answer me, but you're going to need someone to help you. What about your sister? Is she still in Derby? I could call her for you, have her come out here."

No response. Not even a flicker in his eyes or a muscle twitch in his face.

"What about a lawyer? You're gonna need a lawyer, Keith. Is there someone you know that can find one for you?"

Again, nothing.

Peter pulled up to a stoplight and blew out the breath he'd been holding. His shoulders dropped, and he spoke without thinking. "I don't know what happened today, but this isn't you. I've known you since I was in junior high, Keith. Mom used to haul my butt over to your farm to work during the summers. You taught me so much about livestock. Showed me how to build a fence. Taught me to shoot a rifle." He swallowed hard. "You were like a dad to me back then, much better than the one I have, that is. This isn't you."

Silence ensued, and Peter pressed his foot on the accelerator when the light shone green. He was about to give up entirely when a low grumble – almost a growl – came from the backseat. Looking in the mirror again, he noticed Keith staring back at him with dead eyes.

"How the hell did you become sheriff?" Keith asked, his lips barely moving on his expressionless face. "Who in this fine community would vote for – and keep voting for – you? Little Petey Holbrook and his epileptic jitters."

Unexplainable fear crept across Peter's skin at the mention of the bullish nickname the older kids gave him in elementary school. But, Keith couldn't possibly know…

"Peter picked a peck of pickled peppers."

Keith's singsong voice chilled Peter to the core. Another remnant of his childhood – a song the older kids sang to Peter after he had a seizure on the soccer field in third grade, which occurred before Keith moved to Nowhere to take over his family's farm.

"He dropped them all when he had a seizure," Keith continued. "He fell to the ground and crushed them down. And, not a whole pepper was found!'"

The last line echoed in the silence of the car. Peter could not yet explain Keith's lunacy, but how Keith knew these things of his early childhood was a mystery that might never be solved.

"Little Petey Holbrook and his ep-ilep-tic jitters." This time, Keith's laugh was softer and more controlled.

Peter restrained his joy at the sight of the sheriff's station. He couldn't wait to get Keith into a cell, do his paperwork, and go on with his day. Surely Doc Horton could figure out what happened and fix the man, if something could be repaired. Maybe he was broken for good, though Peter couldn't fathom how or why.

After escorting Keith through the side door of the station, Peter turned him left and walked straight back to their booking area. Ollie met them and processed a docile Keith. Fingerprints, photos, and into a cell, their only inmate.

Peter followed Ollie up the stairs and into the front of the station, where Shirley greeted them. Shirley had followed her mom in her career of choice, filling several roles at the sheriff's station since she turned sixteen. Though still in her mid-twenties, she had a tendency to dress on the conservative side, her shirts always buttoned to her neck and skirts flowing around her ankles.

Her blonde hair whipped over her shoulder, her excited eyes full of questions. "What happened out there? Was anyone hurt?"

Her gossiping nature betrayed her otherwise strong work ethic, and Peter had to watch what information he disseminated in her presence. "No one was injured," he said, "but Keith Dusky is in custody on several charges. Can you get Doc Horton over here as soon as he can? I want him to examine Keith." He started to his office, but snapped his fingers. "Can you also call Keith's sister over in Derby? I don't know her number—"

"Don't worry," Shirley said. "I'll call Arlene after I speak to the doctor."

Peter offered a smile as gratitude and continued to his office. He closed the door behind him, grateful for the time alone and the chaos of his morning behind him. Glancing at his watch, he decided to skip lunch despite it being almost noon. Adrenaline still rushed through his system, eliminating his desire for food.

He spent the next hour on his report from the events with Keith. Though nearing the end of the paperwork, he realized he still had another one to write up for Kaylen, as well as meet Doug at the accident site.

Before he could finish reviewing his report on Keith, Ollie poked his head through the door. "Hey, Sheriff."

"Hopefully nothing else has happened," Peter said. "I don't think I can take much more excitement today."

Ollie chuckled and shook his head. "Just wanted to remind you that Doug's waiting for you. He says it's looking like more rain any minute."

"Damn the gray," Peter said. "I may not make it out there before it starts up again, so have him take pictures with his cell phone. The road, tire tracks, impact site. Just everything, even if it doesn't seem significant."

"You got it."

"Can you make a call to Old Bob and see if it was raining out there between one and five this morning? I want to know if that contributed to the accident. See if he happened to hear anything, too."

Old Bob owned the land alongside Old 54 Highway, near where the accident took place. He was well-known, not only for his insomnia, but his weather tracking. Many area farms relied on him more than the Farmer's Almanac for their weather predictions.

Shirley's scream whistled through the air and into Peter's office. He and Ollie didn't hesitate before racing for the door and down the hall, toward the cells from where the shriek originated. As they neared, rhythmic banging filled Peter's ears. Shirley stood several feet away from Keith's cell, her hand on her chest. She turned to Ollie and Peter as they rushed through the door.

Peter ignored her in favor of Keith, whose bleeding forehead crashed into the bars. His crazed laugh had returned, only ceasing when his head rammed into the metal again. Peter struggled with the keys to the cell, but managed to get it open by the third time Keith's skull smashed the bars.

As Keith tumbled out of the cell and onto the floor, blood flew through the air, spattering across Peter's shirt. Ollie rushed over and helped Peter flip Keith to his back. Rivers of crimson flowed down his skin, dripping on the floor. His laugh continued while his vacant eyes stared at the ceiling.

"Call an ambulance!" Peter yelled.

Ollie spoke into his radio, requesting assistance from paramedics.

Shirley paced behind Ollie, her eyes filling with tears. "I just came back to tell him I got ahold of Arlene, and he started laughing and hitting his head. I didn't mean to—"

"You didn't do anything wrong," Peter said. Though he meant every word, he also knew that her hysterics could also make things worse. "Go on up front and wait on those paramedics."

She took off without a response.

Letting out his breath, Peter asked, "What the hell are you trying to do, Keith?"

Keith mumbled something unintelligible under his breath.

Peter leaned over. "What was that?"

The acrid odor of urine filled Peter's nostrils. He glanced toward Keith's jeans in time to see a wet spot spreading across his crotch area, all while Keith continued laughing.

Peter exchanged a glance with Ollie. The lines in Ollie's face deepened as his mouth formed an oval and his nose wrinkled in disgust.

"Coming," Keith said, resuming his chortle.

Peter looked back at Keith. "I don't understand what you're saying."

"They're coming for her," Keith mumbled.

"Who's coming?" Peter asked. "Who are they coming for?"

"They're coming for her," he repeated. "Coming, coming, coming."

"What are you talking about?" Peter asked.

Keith fixed his gaze on Peter, who flinched at the sight of his dark irises. Just an hour ago, Keith's eyes were the same dull blue they'd been his entire life. "Kaylen." His eyes flashed back to blue, and he fell unconscious.

Chapter Five

I s that blood?"

Standing in the empty diner, Peter flinched at Hannah's question, then glanced down at his shirt, to where her finger pointed. He must have had Keith's blood on him the rest of his day after the jail incident without realizing it.

"Are you hurt?" Hannah asked, inching closer to him.

"It's not mine," Peter said, flashing a reassuring smile. "Don't worry."

"Oh, I worry. Can't quite help it where you're concerned." She held her hand out. "Give me the shirt."

"No, you don't have to—"

"Quit being a stubborn mule and give me your shirt." She drew out the last half of the sentence for emphasis.

Peter laughed, a much-needed release from his day. His fingers loosened his tie and worked on his buttons. He stripped the shirt off his shoulders, handed it over, and untucked his white T-shirt to get a bit more comfortable.

"Better give me the tie, too. I'll have them back to you in two days, clean as a whistle."

He relinquished the tie. After Hannah walked into the back of the diner, he slid into the booth next to him, where she had set out iced tea before he arrived. He grabbed the sugar decanter and doctored up his tea to suit his sweet tooth.

Glancing at Hannah's text on his phone again, he couldn't stop the smile his lips formed. *Dinner's heated up for you.* Getting the message from her half an hour earlier had taken his mind off all the difficult events of the day. Hannah never failed to take care of him. If he didn't show up for dinner at the diner, she made sure he ate after hours. Sometimes, she'd go so far as to deliver the food to his house or the station. Between that and penchant for cleaning his uniforms, he wondered if half the town speculated about the two and their lack of an intimate relationship.

She emerged from the kitchen through the swinging doors, two plates of food in her hands. Having skipped lunch, Peter's mouth watered instantly at the sight of the chicken fried steak with steamed broccoli. The comforting aroma of the country gravy reminded him of his mom's biscuits and gravy she made throughout his childhood. She had handed the recipe off to Hannah's dad, who started using it in the diner the day they opened for business.

"Your dinner, Sheriff," Hannah said, setting the plates down on the table, one in front of him, and one on the other side. She climbed into the booth across from him and smiled. "I figured you could use your favorite tonight."

"What makes you say that?" he asked, pushing around his broccoli with his fork like a child with no intention of eating it. As much as he disliked vegetables, Hannah still ensured he received his daily portion.

"Oh, I don't know," she said. "Maybe a little something about Keith Dusky going crazy and trying to kill Wyatt Whitaker, then getting himself locked up in a psych ward in Wichita. Or, could be the car accident this morning with the amnesia girl at the clinic. Take your pick."

"I keep thinking one day I'll wake up in the least gossipin' town in America."

"At least you kept your sense of humor."

Peter stuck a bite of chicken in his mouth and pointed his fork at her. "Can't let that go by the wayside."

"And, to think, with all this goin' on, Fred and Belinda are having a baby." She laughed, her eyes glinting with the same maternal instinct all women seemed to get around the mention of little ones. "Can you imagine? Fred! Having a baby! He wouldn't dare approach a girl for years when we were young, not even in high school."

"Lucky for him, Belinda ain't shy."

"Never woulda guessed he'd be the first of us to get hitched and bring a new one along."

Peter nodded as he munched on a piece of broccoli. He never gave the matter much thought, which one of their childhood friends would marry first and have kids. He knew one day he'd do it himself, but part of him always hoped it would be with Hannah, at least until he became old enough to understand that relationships had to actually *begin* before they went anywhere.

Her voice floated in his ears, rousing him from his deep thoughts. "...the clinic?"

"Hmm?"

She cracked a smile. "The girl? In the clinic?"

"Oh, yeah." He picked up his knife and absently cut into his chicken fried steak. He sectioned off several pieces.

Hannah leaned over the table and spread her hands. "How's she doing?"

"Sorry." He shook his head and set down his utensils. "Kaylen's okay. Just no memory of anything but her name, it seems. She's being released tomorrow morning."

"Kaylen? Unusual name."

"Yeah, I've never heard it before."

Hannah lifted the straw in her tea to her lips. "Where is she going if she can't remember who she is?"

"She'll stay at the inn. Ollie arranged it earlier."

"That's so nice of Delores to take her in like that. The diner can supply her with meals, too."

Peter gazed at her as she sipped her tea. He had memorized her face long ago, somewhere in his years of watching it morph from that of a child to a woman. Looking at her now – the creamy, Irish skin, the brush of coral eyeshadow cascading over soulful green eyes, the freckles smattered across her nose and cheeks – his heart flopped in his chest, a familiar sensation around her.

"Thank you, Hannah," he said. "That means a lot to me for you to help her out like that."

"We can't let the poor girl go hungry."

"We sure can't." His cell phone buzzed on the table, interrupting his moment of peace. Picking it up, he saw Fred's name on the screen. "Hey, Fred! Baby here yet?"

Hannah jumped in her seat across from him, an excited smile lighting her face. Peter waved her off and put the phone on speaker so she could hear.

"Baby..." Fred trailed off.

The tremor in Fred's voice instantly worried Peter. "What's going on?"

"Baby... Born dead."

"What? No... That's not... Where's Belinda?"

"In the room, holdin' our lil un. Baby ain't breathin'."

Peter raised his eyes to Hannah's. Her hand covered her mouth.

"Fred... I'm so... Oh, man. I'm sorry, Fred."

"Baby's dead," Fred said.

The phone disconnected before Peter could say anything else. Without thought, he moved to Hannah's side of the booth. As soon as he scooted next to her, she laid her head on his shoulder. His arms wrapped around her at an awkward angle, and he held her as she cried.

Something behind her caught Peter's attention. A butterfly landed on the rain-soaked window and seemed to stare at him. He couldn't be sure, but it appeared to be the same one from earlier in the day, the one that landed on his nose. Before he could release Hannah to get a closer look, the butterfly flew away. He gripped Hannah tighter and pushed away the dread in his gut.

Chapter Six

S tanding in the lobby of the clinic, Peter dug the heels of his palms into his eyes in an attempt to rub away his fatigue. He had spent the morning catching up on paperwork and reviewing deputy reports along with Wyatt's statement about the dispute with Keith. With Keith's evaluation in a psychiatric hospital in Wichita pending, Peter's part was on hold until he heard from the District Attorney on whether Keith would be institutionalized instead of spending time in jail while awaiting trial for his crimes. Surely the man would plead not guilty by reason of insanity. There was no other explanation.

The call from Doc Horton thirty minutes earlier to pick up Kaylen was just the excuse he had needed to escape his desk. The doctor had said on the phone that her memory hadn't returned, but with no physical ailments, other than the bumps and bruises, she could leave. Peter asked how long it would be for her to remember more than her name, but the doctor had no answers for him.

Lou Ann's friendly chatter caught Peter's attention, and he swiveled around to see her pushing Kaylen in a wheelchair. He smiled at the two, though his emotions ran in the opposite direction. There was no need to let their newcomer experience his anxiousness over the events in his town.

"How are you feeling this morning?" he asked Kaylen.

"Better." She barely glanced at him before averting her eyes, and her timidity from their first meeting carried over into her voice. "Thanks."

Looking at Lou Ann, he asked, "Is there anything I should know? Any medications she needs?"

"Nope," Lou Ann said. "She's good to go. Doc would like to see her in a couple days for a checkup, and to let us know if she starts to remember anything."

"You got it," he said. He started to walk around the wheelchair to take her to his car.

"I can walk." Kaylen's eyes raised up to his, the firmness in them contradicting her quiet voice.

For a moment, he wondered which one represented her true personality: the shy girl who barely spoke, or the confident one hiding behind her unique eyes. "No problem," he said. "Do you need any help?"

"I can do it." She pushed herself up with the arms of the wheelchair, while Lou Ann rushed to her side, her hands out in case Kaylen became unsteady. Kaylen took a few steps forward with Lou Ann by her side, then turned to the kind nurse. "Thank you for everything."

"Of course, honey," Lou Ann said. "You just call if you need me."

Lifting her fingers in a silent goodbye, Kaylen continued walking toward the main doors, which slid open as she approached.

Peter thanked Lou Ann before catching up to the mysterious woman now in his protective custody. He hastened his steps and moved in front of her to hold open the passenger side door of his patrol car parked curbside in the patient loading zone. She climbed into the car, and he waited until she settled in before closing the door.

Once in the driver's seat, he started the engine, but paused before shifting into gear. He looked to his right. Kaylen held her head down, her hands folded neatly in her lap. He figured if he craned his neck to see the floorboard, he'd find her ankles crossed.

The mounting tension in the car bothered Peter. If he hoped to get this girl on her way home, he'd have to question her, which meant gaining her trust... something she didn't seem to give easily.

"I know we've met before, but I'm Sheriff Peter Holbrook, the sheriff of Nowhere County. I'll make sure you're taken care of while we investigate your identity." When she didn't respond, he cleared his throat. "When Doc Horton called me earlier, he said that maybe taking you to see your car could help with your memory. How about we go there?"

She didn't look up, but said, "We can try that."

"Are you hungry? We can stop in at the diner and get you

some lunch first."

"I am."

Peter waited for more, but nothing else came out of her mouth. "Look, Kaylen, this has to be hard on you. Waking up in a hospital, no memory of anything but your name. Now, you're in a car with a stranger who claims to be the sheriff."

Her head lifted, and her gaze swung over to him. He noticed her lips attempting to curl up as if trying to lower her defenses. "It can be a bit unnerving," she said.

He offered her what he hoped was a comforting smile. "Just know that I'm here to help, however you need it. We'll work on this until we find out who you are and where you come from."

She nodded, and her forehead creased. "What if I don't want to find out who I am?"

Tilting his head, Peter asked, "What do you mean?"

She scratched her head near her temple. "I don't know. I just kept... thinking that all night."

"It must be scary not knowing who you are. But, I'm sure there's nothing bad to find."

She looked out the passenger's side window and, under her breath, said, "I hope you're right."

Chapter Seven

They arrived at the diner before lunch but after the breakfast rush, for which Peter was grateful. The few patrons in the diner found Kaylen an instant carnival attraction with her tattoos and unusual eyes. Peter ushered her past the gawkers to the back booth, where he and Hannah had dined the night before.

It only took a minute for Hannah to appear at their table with two waters and silverware. She stuck her hand out to the newcomer. "Hi, hun, good to meet you. I'm Hannah O'Brien."

Kaylen's eyes widened as if overwhelmed at Hannah's friendliness, but she accepted her hand. "Kaylen," she said.

"Well, you're in good hands here with Sheriff Holbrook." Hannah winked in Peter's direction and looked back at Kaylen. "You don't have to worry about a thing, either. The diner will provide all your meals for you, and Delores is going to take care of you over at the inn."

"Um… I don't know what to say." Kaylen's hand reached for her mouth, and she gnawed on her thumbnail.

"Don't have to say a thing," Hannah said. "Oh! Do you have clothes?"

"I…" Kaylen looked at Peter with the question in her eyes. "I don't know if I do or not."

"She doesn't," Peter said. To Kaylen, he said, "You didn't have any bags in your car."

"Well, we can't have you running around in the same clothes day after day! Tell you what, if Peter can bring you back to me after the lunch rush, I'll sneak out. We can hit the boutiques on Main Street. Not that we have many to choose from, but I'm sure we'll find you something."

Kaylen shifted in her seat and lowered her head. "I, uh… thank you for that, but I don't think I have any money."

"Money?" Hannah chuckled. "Don't worry about trivial things like money. I'll take care of you. In fact, Nancy at *Two Times Over* owes me a favor. Goodness knows I donate enough baked goods to her shop for her sales."

"You're so kind," Kaylen said, her voice sincere with a hint of surprise.

"Thanks, Hannah," Peter said as she strutted into the kitchen. She never ceased to amaze him with her generosity. By taking Kaylen off his hands for the afternoon, he could spend some more time looking into her identity without worrying about her being right there if he learned something negative.

Peter snatched a menu from behind the silver napkin dispenser and handed it to Kaylen. "Everything is good here."

"Thank you," she said, accepting the menu. Her eyes roamed around the diner as if searching for something familiar.

"Recognize anything?" he asked.

She shook her head. "Are there any other places to eat in town? Somewhere I may have gone?"

"Our local bar, *The Hole*, but it's not open until late afternoon. I'm not so sure you even made it into town yet to eat. The way your car was found, it looked like you were just crossing over the county line."

Her shoulders heaved with a deep breath, which she let out in a frustrated sigh. "Are there other towns in the area I might have gone to?"

"This is the only town in the county. We can check with other nearby towns, though. They're all larger than Nowhere, but someone may recognize you."

"I guess I'm pretty easy to see coming, huh?"

Peter's gaze fell from her large, bi-colored eyes down to the tattoos on her neck. As he stared at them, he realized they were evenly spaced apart, as if carefully planned. He compared them to the ones on her forearms. Not only were they also perfectly inked on her skin, but some of the symbols on her arms were identical to the ones on her neck.

"You have no idea what any of the tattoos are?" he asked.

"I don't," she said.

"I noticed that some of them are the same."

Before she could respond, Hannah's smiling face appeared at the end of the booth. "Y'all decide what you want?"

Kaylen lifted her menu as if unsure if she wanted to eat anything.

"What do you like to eat?" Hannah asked her. "Maybe I can recommend something."

Kaylen's lips parted, and her brow furrowed as distress consumed her face.

"It's okay," Hannah said, apparently sensing the same thing as Peter. "I can't imagine what you're going through, not remembering anything. I'll bring out two different lunch specials, and you can decide what you like from those plates. Peter will eat just about anything, so he can have what you don't want." She slipped away from the booth, back into the kitchen.

A long moment passed in silence before Kaylen spoke. "Everyone is so nice. Especially your girlfriend."

Peter flinched. "Girlfriend? Who... Oh! Hannah?" A nervous chuckle escaped him. "We're longtime friends, that's all."

A disbelieving smile raised one corner of her mouth, the first hint at her coping with her situation and opening up to him. "Friends," she said. "So, my car..." She trailed off with a question fluctuating her tone.

"Yes, your car. It's out at the McAllister's place. If that doesn't help your memory, we can go to where you had your accident."

"It sure rains here a lot." She gestured to the window, outside of which rain splashed cars in the parking lot. "You probably deal with a lot of accidents."

"It's only this time of year," Peter said. "Locals call it 'the gray.' It's been raining like that every year since long before I was around. But, I'm not sure your accident was caused by the gray. We're still investigating that."

"It sounds so foreboding. 'The gray.' At least you have all those gorgeous butterflies to cut through the dreariness."

Peter's heart skipped a beat, then slammed into his chest. "What butterflies?"

"The ones I saw at the clinic. There seemed to be a lot outside my window while I stayed there. I saw some when we drove here, too."

His hand dropped to the table. How had he missed that? He

hadn't noticed a single one, not at the clinic or on their drive.

"I take it those aren't normal," she said, interrupting his thoughts.

"No. I mean, we do get butterflies here, but not like that. Not so many."

"When did it start?"

The same question entered his mind right before she spoke it. He searched his mind to see if he had any other memories of them, but he already knew the answer. "They started appearing yesterday. After you were in your accident."

She turned to look out the window again. "That doesn't sound good."

"I'm sure it doesn't mean anything." When she didn't reply, Peter reached across the table and gently touched her arm. "Hey, we'll figure this out. Okay?"

She offered a smile and nodded. "Thank you, Sheriff."

"You can call me Peter."

"All right," she said. "Peter."

Chapter Eight

Kaylen's car sat in the same place Peter had left it the day before. He watched as she circled the automobile, carefully examining it inside and out. Her fingers trailed across the impact on the passenger's side, but her creased lips and blank stare remained unreadable. He had thought the seriousness of the crash would give her some emotion – fear, at the very least – but she appeared too intent on remembering something to focus on what her fate might have been.

"Nothing was in the car at all?" she asked. "No registration or insurance?"

"Afraid not."

"You said on the way here that you think someone hit me?"

Peter walked around to the back of the car and pointed out the red paint. "We have a crime scene tech coming out today from Wichita to scrape the paint."

"What will that tell you?"

"Depending on the color, they can tell us what makes and models of vehicles to look for and the years the paint was used. We've already got auto shops in the area looking for red cars with damage matching the accident."

Her eyebrows jetted up. "Wow, that's amazing. Thank you for working so hard—" Her forehead creased, her hand covered her eyes, and she lowered her head.

"Are you okay?"

She moaned softly.

Peter rushed to her side and placed his hand on her shoulder. "Kaylen? Do you need to go to the clinic?"

Her hand fell away, and her squinted eyes locked onto Peter's. "No. A headache just came on suddenly. Doctor said that might happen."

She's lying. Peter wasn't sure what made him think so, but he knew without a doubt she lied about the headache. But, if not that, then what caused her to react like that?

"I'll be fine," she said, forcing a smile. She moved away from him, back to the car. "I wish there had been something here to help me remember something." Looking back at Peter, she said, "Of course, I don't want to impose any more than I already have. I can't ask you to keep carting me around—"

"It's fine," he said. "I don't mind. But, you're right. You need a vehicle to get around." He turned to look at the door to the bays and filled his lungs with the humid spring air. He hated to bother Fred, not when he had just suffered such a huge loss the night before, but he always had extra cars around to use as loaners for his customers.

He jerked his head in the direction of the door. "Let's go see Fred. His house is up on the hill behind the shop, and he should have a car you can borrow while we work on that memory of yours. You okay to walk?"

"Yeah, of course." She started toward him. "I think it will do me good to get some more walking in. You really think Fred would just let me use a car? He doesn't know me." she asked as they left the bays and moved along the trail behind the building

"Fred would give you his house if he thought it would help. He's just one of those guys."

"I guess I had an accident in the right town," she said with a small laugh. "I don't know what I did to deserve so much support, but I'm grateful."

While he enjoyed the conversation with Kaylen, and that she was being more open with him, he noticed her "headache" had cleared up quickly, reaffirming his earlier suspicion that she lied. She hadn't faked the pain, though; something happened, but it wasn't what she'd said.

"It's up here," Peter said, gesturing to their left. He followed her up the hill, along the makeshift wooden steps half-buried in the ground.

"Not much of a hill," Kaylen said.

"You're in Kansas. Our speedbumps are considered

mountains."

Her unrestrained laughter filled the air, warming Peter's heart with its genuine amusement. With her starting out the day so shy, he didn't know she had it in her, but she seemed to be coming around and trusting him more.

"Is this town really called 'Nowhere'?"

"Sure is," Peter said. They reached a wider part of the path, and he caught up so they walked side-by-side. "Honestly, no one really knows where the name came from. Ask the locals, and they'll each tell their version of the town's history. The stories keep getting twisted as they're passed down through the generations, and they seem to multiply in numbers, too."

"It's a great name for a town," she said. "It feels… authentic small-town. Like whoever came up with it really thought it through. Nowhere, but somewhere. Smart, yet humorous."

"I've never given the name much thought." Peter laughed, and she joined in. "You must have been every student's nightmare in English class when it came to dissecting symbolism."

"If I could remember, I'd be able to tell you." She punctuated her sarcasm with more laughter.

Peter shook his head as they walked up the steps to Fred's bungalow. Now that she had opened up to him, relief flowed through him. She would be much easier to work with during the investigation into her past than he thought.

She stopped walking on the rickety porch, causing him to turn around. "Look," she said, pointing to the front door. In front of the screen, just above a small hole, a butterfly fluttered its bright blue wings outlined in black.

"What in the world?" He stared at the insect, but his gut twisted as he wondered why it was there at that precise moment.

"Something's wrong."

Kaylen's words resonated in his ears, and he stepped up to the door. "What makes you say that?" he asked.

"I don't know."

He opened the screen and discovered the front door ajar. Pushing it open, he inched inside. "Fred? Belinda? Y'all here?"

No answer.

The thick aroma of beef stew hit him as he entered the front hallway. "I think they're in the kitchen," he said. He turned into the small dining room, which connected to the kitchen. "Belinda? Fred?"

He moved across the linoleum floor and cracked open the lid to a crockpot on the counter, which contained their slow-cooking dinner.

"Sheriff!"

He hesitated, not realizing Kaylen had wandered off. He moved back into the hall and toward the living room, from where her voice originated. Rounding the corner, he stopped short and sucked in his breath. Slumped over the coffee table, crimson dripping down the wood legs and onto the matted, brown carpet, Belinda's glassy eyes stared into the distance, a bullet wound on the side of her head. Fred's legs jutted out from between the couch and recliner.

Peter ran past Kaylen to reach Fred. He pushed the floor lamp aside and knelt next to his friend, who gasped shallow breaths. Pressing his fingertips to Fred's bloody neck, he found a light pulse. "Hang in there," Peter said. He pressed the button on the radio mic mounted on the left side of his chest. "I need an ambulance at the McAllister's place right away."

He heard Shirley's voice through the radio, but focused instead on Fred's lips, which attempted to move. Lowering his head, he asked, "What was that?"

"Baby's dead." He emitted a gurgling sound, a soft moan, then fell silent.

"Fred?" Peter's own breathing stopped as he checked for signs of life. "Fred, come on."

A hand draped over Peter's shoulder. Somewhere in his mind, he knew it was Kaylen behind him, but he didn't want to give up on Fred just yet.

"He's not breathing," Kaylen said.

Peter tilted back Fred's head to start CPR, but his eyes caught view of Fred's previously white T-shirt and the multiple holes where bullets had ripped through it. There was no hope for reviving Fred. He glanced down at his own uniform, now covered in blood – the second day in a row.

He rose and went to Belinda. Though he already knew she was dead, he wanted to check on her. Who had come into their home and massacred them, two staples of the community who had never harmed a soul? Two of his closest friends, and just after the death of their baby.

As he double-checked for a pulse, just in case, his gaze traveled down Belinda's right arm, which had fallen over the side of the coffee table. His stomach twisted at the sight of the gun dangling from her fingertips, her index finger still covering the trigger.

Chapter Nine

Y ou knew them well?"

Kaylen's question rang in Peter's ears. After giving her statement to the Detective Sergeant Kirk Carlson, who arrived with the crime scene technicians from Wichita, Peter excused them so he could take her back to the diner, away from the excitement. He promised to return after changing out of his blood-soaked uniform so they could complete the initial investigation.

"Peter... I'm sorry about your friends."

He kept his eyes on the road. "Fred was the closest friend I have. Besides Hannah, I suppose."

Silence followed as he drove toward the diner on slick streets. The gray had taken hold of the city shortly after he found Fred and Belinda's bodies, and the rain crashed on the ground harder than it had during the past few days. He never believed the gray to be an omen, never believed in omens at all, but now it seemed a predictor of things to come. Like the butterflies...

His thoughts froze on the word. Pulling up to a red light, he shifted his gaze to Kaylen. "What was it about the butterfly on the door that made you think something was wrong?"

She returned his stare, her brows knitted and eyes squinted. "The butterfly means something, but I'm not sure—" Her hand flew up to her forehead as a pained moan escaped her.

He grabbed her arm. "Are you okay?"

She held up her other hand, but didn't raise her head. "I don't... I think so. Just these headaches."

"Have you had many? Other than the one earlier, that is."

Nodding, she said, "A few. They started this morning, before

I left the clinic."

"What did Doc Horton say?"

"He didn't…" She dropped her hand and glanced at Peter, guilt in her eyes. "I didn't tell him."

"We have to call him. Something could be wrong."

"No, I don't think anything's wrong. I really don't want to go back to the clinic."

He started to say something else, but she interrupted him.

"I think the light's been green for a while."

His neck snapped around to look at the light, which turned yellow just as his shoe touched the accelerator. He lifted his foot off the pedal and returned it to the brake, grateful for another moment to talk to Kaylen about her symptoms. "This is more than headaches, isn't it?"

She rubbed her temples. "I think my memories are trying to come back. I didn't know it would be like this, though. And, it's weird. It's as if…" She grimaced as pain overcame her.

Peter grasped her tattooed forearm. "What can I do?"

Adjusting herself in the seat and sitting up straight, she shook her head.

"What do you remember?"

"The butterfly. All the butterflies. So many of them…"

He let go of her arm and gripped the steering wheel, his palms twisting over the top with nervous energy.

"The light's green again."

His foot responded to her words by pressing down the accelerator. "We can go to the clinic," he said. "It's no problem."

"I'll be fine." Her words came out easy, as if the headache she claimed moments ago was already cleared. She rotated her head to look out the window. "The headache will go away."

Returning his gaze to the road ahead, he wondered again if there was no headache. She had tried to tell him something else about the memories, but the pain cut her off. *If it really is pain*, he thought. Something deep in his gut, the same nagging instinct that attacked him during her last episode, said she was lying.

A few minutes later, he pulled his car alongside the curb a few doors down from the diner. "I, uh…" He looked down at the blood on his uniform. "I can't go in like this. Just go find Hannah, and she'll take care of you for the afternoon."

"I'm sorry again about your friends," Kaylen said.

The reality of Fred and Belinda's deaths dried out his mouth and threatened to choke tears from him. "Please, don't tell Hannah anything. I need to tell her myself."

"I won't," she said. She opened the passenger door and slipped out of the car without another word.

Peter watched her walk toward the diner, head down. She peeked over her shoulder at him, then pulled the door open and disappeared. He drove off before anyone could catch a glimpse of him and notice the blood soaking his clothes.

At his home, he carefully stripped off his clothing and placed it into a paper sack. He didn't know if the Wichita police would want it as part of their investigation and wanted to ensure the survival of any DNA evidence. It didn't matter much whether they wanted it. Hannah might be great at getting out some stains, but this one was ruined for good.

Chapter Ten

W alking up to Fred and Belinda's bungalow would never again be the same, Peter realized as he maneuvered through the police officers around the scene. He spied Detective Sergeant Kirk Carlson near the front door of the dead couple's home and made his way over to him.

Kirk shot a strained smile at him. "I'm sure sorry about all this, Peter."

"Yeah, me, too." He offered up the brown grocery sack with his clothes in it. "I didn't have an official evidence bag at home, but here is my uniform if you need it for the investigation."

"Sure, we'll take it in." He took the bag and looked past Peter. "Ted?" He waved over a crime scene technician, who handed Peter a chain of custody form.

Once Peter signed the form, he asked, "Ready for my statement?"

"Wanna walk while we do this?" Kirk asked, taking a small notepad out of his pocket.

Peter led him down the walkway, toward the vehicle bays. He detailed out his arrival, their venture into the bays, and what happened when they went inside the house.

"Do you normally just walk into their home?" Kirk asked as they stood outside.

"Yeah, it's pretty common. He does the same at mine. Plus, the door was open a bit already."

"How far was it open?"

"Just a few inches. Like someone forgot to shut it all the way." Peter stopped walking when they reached the back of the bays. He couldn't help but glance down at the spot where Fred had thrown his cigarette the day before. Just one of many memories that he'd have to hold close.

He choked back his grief and asked, "How much longer do you think it will take to finish up here?"

"Couple hours at the most. It's pretty cut and dried."

"Is it at all possible that someone came in, shot them both, then arranged it to look like a murder-suicide?"

"Blood spatter doesn't support it. They died where you found them. Neither one of them was moved. Of course, we'll check the angle of the bullets and the tattooing around the entry wounds to confirm distance of the gun and where it was held when they were shot, but I don't think we'll find anything to support another shooter."

"But, is it still possible? Maybe someone came in, and he forced them into their current positions?" Peter knew the answers, but the hope swelling in his heart wouldn't let it go.

"I don't see any other way it could have happened," Kirk said. "We checked for gunshot residue, and it's on her right hand. He has none on his."

"I can't believe that. I mean, I know what you're saying, and if it were anyone else, I'd agree. But, this is Fred and Belinda."

"How long have you known them?"

"Fred and I have been friends since I moved to Nowhere. Second grade. Belinda's grandpa passed away ten years ago. Her parents inherited the house, but she came to live here by herself when she was in her early twenties. Before that, she was up north in Hays. It wasn't but a year later that she moved in with Fred."

"And, they had a good relationship?"

"The best. Never heard them argue. Even if they disagreed, they always had smiles on their faces." Something popped into Peter's memory. "The slow-cooker."

"I'm sorry?"

"Belinda had put on a stew. Why would she do that if she was going to do... this?"

"Could it have been Fred?"

"No, no. Fred couldn't boil an egg. Belinda did all the cooking."

"People do strange things before... well, you know. You said they just lost a baby. Did she blame him? Blame herself? Couldn't live with what happened?"

"I don't know. I just don't know."

"It's tough to see things when you're so close to someone." Kirk sighed. "You said the door was ajar when you got here. Is that why you went inside?"

Peter shook his head. "No one locks their doors out here. Maybe the homes on Main Street, but out here and out where I live, doors are always open. I just figured Fred left it open. He is… was always a bit absentminded."

"Then, what made you go inside?"

"There was a…" He almost said "butterfly," but stopped himself. *How strange would that sound?* he thought. He couldn't have the detective thinking he'd lost his mind.

"A what?" Kirk asked.

"Just a bad feeling."

"I get that."

Eager to change the subject, Peter said, "While your guys are here, can they scrape the paint from Kaylen's car? Someone was coming out in the next day to do it anyway."

"What's the story with the car?"

"Hit-and-run, allegedly. We have a small dent in the back of her car with some foreign red paint."

"Allegedly?" Kirk cocked his head to the side. "Wouldn't she know if she were hit?"

"Seems she's got a bit of amnesia."

"Well, then, I guess she wouldn't know. Yeah, we can get that done today. Are you having any luck in her identity?"

"None." Hands shoved in pockets, Peter absently kicked the dirt around his feet.

"I haven't seen her face come across as a missing person or anything."

"I haven't sent it over to you yet." At Kirk's confused look, he added, "To be honest, I was a little worried about this whole hit-and-run thing. I don't know if someone tried to run her off the road purposely or if it was an accident. Things like that just don't happen 'round here."

"Yeah, that's a bit sticky. Let me know if you need help sorting it out. I'll have Ted come over to scrape that paint for you when we're done at the house." He gestured to the vehicle bays. "Don't suppose the car happens to be in here? Save us a trip somewhere else?"

Peter waved for Kirk to follow him. "It's your lucky day. Follow me."

Chapter Eleven

For the first time that day, as he sat in the dark of his patrol car in front of the diner, Peter allowed numbness to wash over him. Eventually, and soon, he'd have to deal with the tragedy of Fred and Belinda. In this moment, though, he preferred the tingling of his nerves, the emotional detachment that protected him – no, *saved* him – from having to experience grief. Maybe once Kaylen was safely tucked away at the inn and he rested quietly in his home, the sorrow would overcome him. He would have to figure out how to emotionally cope with it then.

Staring at the diner door, he wondered what he would say to Hannah. So far, the news of the murder-suicide had remained quiet. If it had traveled around town, she would have called his phone until he answered. That conversation was best left for face-to-face, and the time had unfortunately arrived.

He shoved open his car door, his boots sloshing into a puddle when they hit the street. The rain splashed onto the ankles of his pants, coating his already soured mood with frustration. Car locked, he made his way inside the closed diner, where Hannah and Kaylen waited for him, both wearing curious expressions. When Hannah had texted him a few hours earlier to know when to expect him, he had responded *Not long*. Though his intention was to finish up his report on the McAllisters at his office and head out, his thoughts had snared him in a bear trap. Before he knew it, he had procrastinated working on the report for over two hours.

"I know," he said before Hannah could berate him for his tardiness. He gestured toward the shopping bags on the floor next to Kaylen. "Looks like you two had fun today."

"Full afternoon of shopping, then dinner here." Hannah pointed at him. "Which you missed, by the way."

"I'm sorry," Peter said. "You know how it gets some days."

"Yeah, well, I have leftovers for ya." She slid off the stool and sauntered toward the kitchen.

"Did you enjoy yourself?" Peter asked Kaylen as he rested on the stool next to her.

Her eyelids lifted, revealing the full size of her bi-colored eyes. "Hannah's amazing," she said. "She's been so kind to me without any real reason."

"That's Hannah's way. Always welcoming and accommodating to everyone who comes across her."

"Well, I'm grateful to her, and you, also."

Peter chuckled. "I've not done anything more than drop you off into Hannah's capable hands. And, now, I'm going to drop you off with Delores at the inn."

"Exactly," she said, a warm smile claiming her lips.

"Okay," Hannah said, emerging from the kitchen's swinging doors, a white, plastic bag in her hand. "Tonight, you're having a French dip with extra au jus, French fries, and a side of steamed veggies."

He smiled at her insistence of supplying him with vegetables, stood up, and accepted the food. "Thank you once again. We better let you get closed up here."

Kaylen slipped off the stool. "I can never thank you enough," Kaylen said, collecting her bags.

"Don't say another word," Hannah said, waving her hand. "It's what we do here. Anything you need, you have my number."

"I'll pick her up in the morning and bring her by for breakfast," Peter told Hannah.

"I'll save you a booth." Hannah shifted from side-to-side. "Um, Peter? Rodney Barrow drove by the McAllister's place earlier. Said there were a lot of police cars there, maybe an ambulance, but he couldn't see much 'cause the trees block their house. I know you said someone was stopping off for something on Kaylen's car, but is everything okay?"

Peter's hands trembled, his thoughts lost in a whirlwind of ways to tell Hannah.

Before he could recover, Hannah must have picked up on his reluctance and downtrodden emotions. "What's going on?"

He turned to Kaylen. "Do you mind waiting in my car? It's parked right out front." He dug the keys out of his pocket and handed them to her.

She said her goodbyes to Hannah and exited the diner.

As soon as the door shut, Hannah's expression hardened. "Peter Holbrook, you tell me what's going on right now. I don't know why, after all these years, you think you can hide something from me—"

"Fred and Belinda are gone." The words left a hollow echo in the diner and an acrid taste on his tongue.

"What?" She stepped back, her hand on her chest. "What... what are you saying? Where did they go?"

"Hannah..." He placed his hand on her upper arm. "I'm so sorry."

Her chin trembled uncontrollably. "What... what happened? Where? How?"

Peter didn't answer, only dropped his food bag on the ground and gathered her into his arms. Her body shuddered against him, and the moisture on her cheek penetrated the material of his uniform, dampening his shoulder. She didn't need to hear the details tonight. She had enough to process.

He had no idea how much time had passed when she loosened her grip around his waist. Staring up at him, her eyes longing for comfort, she whispered, "What are we going to do?"

"I don't know," he said. He wished he had an answer for her, but he could barely think, let alone come up with words to soothe her pain.

"Oh, no! Kaylen's in your car! This whole time—"

"It's okay," he said. "This is more important right now."

"Well, let's not neglect the poor girl. I mean... we can—" A tearful laugh interrupted her. "I don't know what the hell I mean."

"Do you want to come over to my place after I drop off Kaylen and you close up? We can talk and—"

"No, no," she said, wiping her cheeks. "I don't need to burden you tonight, and I'm probably better off alone anyway." She sniffed and brushed the tears from her cheeks. "Tomorrow. We can talk then."

"You're sure?"

Her nod ended the discussion.

He leaned into her and kissed her cheek, lingering longer than he should for a friendly gesture. "Call me if you need to."

At her silence, he exited the diner and stepped into the thick of the gray. A gust of bitter wind threatened to blow the trees down around him. He slapped his hand down on top of his hat before it could fly away. Head down, he rushed around his patrol car to the driver's side. Thick drops pelted him from a slanted angle, soaking him through to his chilled bones.

"It's getting much worse out there," Kaylen said when he settled into his seat. Her squinted eyes peered out the windshield.

His seatbelt clicked as he secured it, and his gaze darted to the side to make sure she had hers on as well. The windshield wipers sprung to life with the engine, but visibility remained low, even under the flood of his headlights.

"Does it always get this bad?" she asked.

"Every year." He shifted into drive and steered the car onto the main road.

"Was it like this when I wrecked?"

"It stormed a lot that night, but I don't know the exact weather conditions at the time of your accident. The roads must have been slick, though."

"I wish I could remember. Just one thing."

The melancholy in her words touched his soul. Already, the stranger had worked her way into their lives, as if she'd always been part of the town. Hannah had thrown a protective wing over her new friend, and Peter shared that instinct to watch over her, to help her discover her past. Something about Kaylen... she *belonged* there somehow. Her presence made sense. But, she had just arrived a day earlier, and not purposefully. If she hadn't been in the accident, if she hadn't lost her memory, she wouldn't have stuck around. No one stayed in Nowhere for long.

He refocused his attention to the slick roads and their destination of the inn. When he pulled up to the curb in front of the restored Victorian mansion that served as the town's only hotel, he shifted the car into park and turned to Kaylen.

"We're here," he said, but she continued to stare out the window at the inn. "Let me help you with your things."

"It's okay," she said. "Hannah drove me here earlier and introduced me to Delores." She reached into her pocket, retrieved a hotel keycard, and waved it at him.

"I should have known she took care of that, too."

"I can't get over how beautiful this is. Has it always been an inn?"

"Delores didn't give you the tour?"

She shook her head. "We were in a bit of a hurry."

"Don't ask her any questions tonight, then. She'll keep you up half the night talking about the history of this place."

A restrained laugh bubbled out of her. "Thanks for the warning."

"The short version is the inn was built in 1894 and was originally used as a hospital. It was repurposed over the years. A school building, then a private home. Eventually, it was deemed historical and became what it is today."

"So long as you don't tell me it's haunted, I'm good."

"Many people have tried to claim there are ghosts of those patients who died back then. Either that, or it's the ghost of the man who built the home. We've even had our share of ghost researchers out here. Hopefully that's not why you came to town."

"To find ghosts?" She grimaced. "I doubt it. At least, I don't feel like a ghost chaser."

"Good thing. I'd sure hate to have to run you out of town." He winked at her before he could stop the gesture he thought was only reserved for Hannah. He cleared his throat and busied himself with getting a business card out of his wallet. Writing his cell number on the back of the card, he said, "Your room should have a phone—"

"Hannah bought me one, too."

"She really thought of everything. If you need something, give me a call. I'm heading back to the station to do some work, and it's less than a mile away. I'll pick you up for breakfast at seven."

The upward curve of her lips lit up her shadowed face with graciousness. "See you in the morning then." The passenger door swung open, and she climbed out of the car. "What in the world?"

Something in her voice dragged him from the car as well. He peered over the roof and froze. Butterflies danced near the front door to the inn, as if expecting Kaylen's arrival.

Her head twisted to the side, her mouth agape, and she swung her gaze to meet his.

Peter shrugged and walked around the car until he stood next to her. He had no explanation for anything that had happened the past two days, certainly not one for the sudden influx of activity from butterflies in his town.

"What do you think it is?" she whispered, as if the insects could hear. "I didn't think they came out in the rain."

"They don't." He watched as they stayed within their bounds, just under the front awning, not allowing any drops of rain to push them to the ground.

Without another word, Kaylen's feet moved in the direction of the butterflies. When she reached them, they encircled her. Hands in the air, she turned around and let loose an innocent, playful laugh.

He smiled at the hypnotizing sight. These butterflies, like all the others, didn't behave the way nature dictated. They had purpose.

Just like Kaylen, Peter thought. They belonged here as much as she did.

Kaylen stepped back into the gray, rain assaulting her already soaked clothing. "I need to get inside and out of these clothes."

He nodded and retrieved her bags from the car. "Hot shower will take the chill from your bones."

"I'll see you in the morning," she said, taking her items from him.

He tipped his hat at her and waited until she passed through the inn's door before going back to his car.

Chapter Twelve

P eter's eyelids slipped closed again, and he shook himself awake. Glancing at his watch, he groaned at the late hour. He hadn't intended to spend so much time at the station that night, but work kept him grounded in his chair. Reports from his deputies, a quarterly budget to review for the political side of the county, and a handful of résumés for an empty deputy position… all his usual workload gotten away from him in the storm that hit them the moment Kaylen came into town, as if her arrival triggered everything. Not that she caused it, but her presence somehow seemed tied to the events.

He hated to think that, chided himself for the idea, but he couldn't deny it. Nowhere had always run smoothly. Each day, he could rely on the ordinary and average. Doors stayed unlocked, crime stayed away, and some of the townsfolk didn't even have Internet. Life moved to its own clock. No one under his jurisdiction was equipped for the events they had faced. And, none of it had happened until she came to town.

The tattoos stuck in his mind. He decided to sketch what he remembered on a blank page of his notepad. *Definitely symbols*, he thought as he visualized the images. If he could get them on paper, he could search online for their origin. But, as soon as he touched the tip of the pen to draw, the symbols vanished in his mind, and every attempt to recall them failed.

Frustrated, he tossed the pen on his desk. It skidded across his work and tumbled off the edge.

"Everything okay, boss?"

Peter looked up to see Deputy Len Carter walking into the

office.

"You dropped something." Len bent over and returned to view with the runaway pen twirling between his fingers.

"Thanks," Peter said, taking the pen and placing it in the mug with other writing utensils. "I didn't know you were working tonight."

"I traded shifts. My cousin's wedding is next weekend."

"That's right. I was just getting out of here. Unless you needed me?"

"Wanted to check on the girl," Len said.

"The accident victim?" Peter asked. "She's doing much better."

"Heard she was staying at the inn. Lucy thought she'd make her a meal or something." Len's wife always cooked for the infirmed.

"That sounds nice. Right now, her meals are covered at the diner."

"Hannah's good like that." Len shifted back and forth. "The girl got her memory back?"

"Not yet," Peter said, a little exasperated with the questions. He'd received at least a hundred of them from deputies and, of course, Shirley. He shut down his computer and stood up. "I'm heading on home, if there's nothing else."

"No, no, Sheriff. You go on. Late night for ya."

Peter's cell phone rang, and he answered it despite the unknown number. "Sheriff Hol—"

"Peter?"

The raspy voice sounded somewhat familiar, but he couldn't place it immediately. "Who is… Kaylen?"

"Someone's in my room."

"In your room?" He exchanged a glance with Len. "Where are you exactly?"

"Bathroom. Locked in. They're trying to open it."

"Stay on the phone with me. We're coming now." He held the phone away from his ear and signaled to Len to follow him out the door. "Someone's breaking into Kaylen's room."

"Peter! Hurry!" Her terrified voice seeped into his ears.

Every muscle in his body tensed before springing into action. "I'm coming." He raced out the back door with Len in tow. "I'm not far." Once they made it inside the car, he started the engine while Len flipped on the lights and sirens.

His phone connected with the Bluetooth in his car, and Kaylen's hushed voice filled the vehicle. "I think they're almost in."

Peter's mind raced. "Is there a window?"

"I'm on the second floor."

He cursed under his breath. "Do you know how many people there are?"

"Sounds like one."

They rounded the corner, but the inn was still several blocks away.

"I think he's got the lock!"

"Yell out that the police are on their way." It was risky and ill-advised, but he didn't know any other way. Whoever it was had already made it in the room. If they had opened the lock to the bathroom, she had little other choice.

He listened as she repeated his warning in a loud, firm voice.

The patrol car pulled up alongside the inn, and both he and Len dashed out of the car. "Go out back in case they went that way," he said to Len. He removed his gun from its holster and mashed the phone against his ear. "What room?"

"203."

Gripping his gun, he entered the inn, but saw no one in the foyer. He bounded up the carpeted stairs and carefully made his way down the hall until he reached the slightly ajar door to her room. "I'm right outside," he whispered into the phone. "I'm hanging up."

With his cell phone secured in his back pocket, he carefully pushed the door open with the toe of his boot and entered. It was a standard layout for the inn: a four-post bed to his left, a connecting bathroom, and a window bay with a quaint sitting area in front of him. The open floor plan allowed for him to quickly clear it. Her warning must have scared off the intruder.

"Kaylen? You can come out."

She exited the bathroom, her wide eyes darting around. Her brow knitted as she neared him. Between shallow breaths, she asked, "Are you sure it's safe?"

"I'm positive."

She blew out her breath and sidled up to him, still looking around the room as if she expected to see the intruder. "Did you find whoever it was?"

"One of my deputies is looking out back. I didn't see anyone else." His palm landed on her upper arm, and he tilted his head to catch her gaze. "Are you okay?"

"Yeah," she said.

"No one out there," Len said, walking into the room. "I searched back and front, but nothing. Well, ran into Delores, but she said she didn't hear anything. Told her to wait in her room."

Seeing Len reminded Peter of the earlier questions about Kaylen – questions he had heard from so many people over the past few days. Everyone wanted to know everything about her, and any one of them might leak information to whoever was after her. He had to somehow ensure her safety.

"Can you find out if there are any other guests who may have heard something?" Peter asked. He didn't believe the inn had any other occupants, but he wanted to give a viable excuse for Len to leave.

"Sure thing," Len said, shrugging, "but I doubt it on a Tuesday."

As soon as Len left, Peter turned to Kaylen. "Get your stuff together."

"Where are we going?"

"Not sure, but somewhere else."

"Someone ran me off the road, didn't they?"

There was no point in lying or even hinting otherwise. "I think that's a safe assumption."

She took a small step back. Her lips pursed, and her contemplating eyes inspected the plush carpet around her bare feet.

"I'm sorry." His words seemed hollow in the shadow of the situation. His inadequacy overcame him. They were a small town, completely unequipped and easily intimidated in the face of real crime. Those things that never happened in Nowhere.

"I'll get my things."

Peter lowered himself in the chair next to the bay window, considering his next moves while Kaylen bustled around the room. He intended to hand her off to the Wichita Police Department, leaving her in the capable hands of Detective Sergeant Kirk Carlson and others. Though he trusted Kirk, he decided against the idea, fearing she would soon become lost in their caseload. A larger city provided ample opportunity for whoever hunted her to disappear in the crowds, remaining unseen until they struck. Whatever stranger had followed her into town and lurked, waiting to strike when she was alone, would stand out more in Nowhere.

But, where to take her?

He pondered that question as they exited her room and rode the elevator down to the first floor in silence.

The doors slid open just as Len walked in front of them. The lanky deputy turned and stepped back. "Well, hey there, Sheriff. Delores said no other guests."

"Thanks," Peter said, shifting Kaylen's bags to his left hand so he could get his car keys out of his pocket. "Do me a favor and sit on Kaylen's room until morning. I want to make sure no one else tries to break in. I'll call Detective Carlson to have a forensics team come out."

"What if a call comes in? Should I leave?"

"I'll have it directed to Ollie. He's on call tonight."

"What about Kaylen? Where's she staying? Do we need someone to watch her?"

Kaylen's eyes bored into the side of Peter's face, and he looked down at her. "I'll get her relocated, and then I can reassess her situation tomorrow."

Len tipped his hat and walked past them, into the elevator cab.

Kaylen trailed behind Peter through the lobby. He held open the front door for her. As they stepped into the night, the sky spat little drops of rain on them, as if the gray refused to let go. It seemed much worse this season than most. Another thing that started when Kaylen arrived in their town, he thought as she climbed into his car. He shut the door behind her and moved to the driver's side, his thoughts biting him like chiggers in a dense field. It sounded as if he were blaming her for not only the gray, but all the tragedy that ensued, ludicrous as it was.

The car engine turned over, and he rubbed his chilled hands together.

"Where am I going?"

Her question broke through his thoughts. He still had no answer for her sleeping situation. Except...

"I have a guest room."

"Your house?"

Though a last-minute idea, it made sense. "It's the only place I can think of this late where you'll be safe. Tomorrow, we can find somewhere else."

"Okay."

"That was… easy." He threw the transmission into drive and

pulled away from the curb.

"Like you said, there aren't many options this time of night. I'm not sure where else I'd feel safe, either."

They sat in silence on the way to his house until they passed the "Now Leaving Nowhere" sign.

"You don't live in Nowhere?" Kaylen asked.

"I live in Nowhere County, just not inside the town limits."

"I see."

"One of the reasons I thought you'd be safer with me for tonight. Twenty-two acres of pure country bliss. All the gossiping neighbors are beyond shouting distance."

"Must be wonderful."

He pulled the car under the carport alongside his farmhouse, parking it just behind his beat-up pickup truck, the epitome of a country boy. She followed him around to the front and up the wood steps. While she glanced around the large porch, he opened the door.

"No locks?" she asked him as they moved indoors.

"We have 'em, but don't use them much. Especially out here. No reason to." A thought struck him. "You must not live in a small town if you find that odd."

Her eyebrows arched, and she shrugged. "Then, maybe I'm from a city." Looking around his large foyer and up the dark wood stairs, she said, "This is nice."

"Thanks." He took his gun out of its holster and removed his duty belt, hanging it on the hook by the front door. "I did most of the remodeling myself when I bought it some years back. Wanted to keep the country in it without all the red and white checks or apples and roosters everywhere. It's always needing some work, but it's livable."

He motioned for her to follow him into the living room. Gesturing to the left, he said, "Kitchen's that way. Not much in it, but you're welcome to whatever you find. Guest room is off the main hall over here." He led her to the room, pointing out the bathroom along the way.

She set her bag down on the quilt-covered queen bed. "This is perfect. I feel much safer here."

"Good," he said. "I know it's late, but would you like something to drink?"

"Water sounds great."

After he filled up two glasses with ice water, they settled down on the couch in the living room. "How are you doing?" he asked. "I know that must have been a little traumatic for you."

"Surprisingly okay. I mean, it scared me at first. But, then…" Her shoulders heaved with a large breath that she let out in a half-laugh. "I don't quite know what I'm feeling."

"Adrenaline," he said. "It does strange things to a person."

"Adrenaline." She nodded and clasped her hands together in her lap. "Okay. At least I'm not crazy, 'cause it feels a bit like I'm losing my mind right now."

"Hey, no, don't say that."

"I thought I was imagining it and—"

"You weren't imagining the break-in."

"It just seems like with this damned amnesia that… I don't know." She threw her hands up and exasperation wrinkled the skin around her eyes and mouth. "Maybe my mind is not all there." She averted her gaze to the floor.

"Is there something I should know?" he asked as he sat next to her.

She swallowed hard and shifted in her seat. "I think my memories are becoming a bit clearer."

His posture straightened. "Like what?"

"Nothing specific. It's strange, really. It's not like I thought it would be, either."

"How do you mean?"

"I'm not sure, exactly. I thought maybe I'd see images from my past flash in my head. Or, a small thread of a memory would appear, and then I would tug on it until it unraveled."

"How are they coming back?"

"I'm seeing pictures, things from the past. Strange things, though. It's like they're not real. Then there's the…" A disbelieving laugh rolled out of her, and she shook her head. "I don't even know how to explain this."

"What is it?"

"Nothing," she said, finality riding the syllables. Her mouth clamped shut, and she folded her hands.

"You know, there's no manual to getting your memory back after a trauma like that. I'm sure whatever you're experiencing is completely normal."

She lifted her gaze to his face, her damp eyes revealing her vulnerability. "It doesn't feel like it."

"We can call Doc Horton if—"

"No. I don't want him to think I'm crazy and lock me up or something."

"I can promise you he won't do that, but I can understand. You don't know him. Hard to trust someone you don't know."

"I trust you."

Her words hung in the air between them as they studied each other. An unspoken and uninvited attraction he failed – *refused* – to acknowledge before then swelled in his chest. He wanted to break their stare, but a part of him held on. The conversation wasn't over just yet.

"My turn to be honest with you." The statement slipped out before he could think twice. "I don't know why. Not even sure I should be saying this."

She tilted her head, and curiosity consumed her face.

"Ever since you arrived…" He trailed off as he formed his words. "I think… no, I *know* that you belong here. I can't explain it, and it makes absolutely no sense. But, it's like you are supposed to be here. In this town. Right at this moment."

Her lips parted to allow for a small gasp. Slowly, she nodded and looked away. "I think you're right, but I don't know why either."

He scooted to the edge of the couch and inched a little to his right, closer to her. "Something is going on in this town. I've always known that our town was a little off. That something wasn't right, especially when the gray came. But, now…" His jaw clenched as he thought about all the loss they had suffered. "Something is very wrong, and I don't know how to fix it. I don't know how to protect everyone from what's happening. I don't know how to protect you."

"Maybe you're not supposed to."

He flinched at her quiet words. As an adult, he had always played that role, the protector. The one people turned to in times of need. The problems of their town had been miniscule in comparison to what they experienced the last two days, but he still watched over the townsfolk and kept them from harm. At least, he thought he did. Maybe he wasn't as good at his job as he thought. Certainly, not in the face of so much adversity.

But, then again, maybe Kaylen was right.

Chapter Thirteen

The morning aroma of fresh-brewed coffee guided Peter down the stairs, through the living room, and into his kitchen. He couldn't think of the last time his coffeemaker had any purpose in his home other than dusty kitchen décor. He left those things up to the professionals, Hannah and Shirley.

"Good morning." Kaylen's voice greeted him before he saw her. Her head popped up from behind the open refrigerator door, a warm smile passing over her lips. "You don't seem to have much to eat here."

"The diner is my kitchen," he said.

"For everything?"

"Every meal I manage to sneak in."

"Something tells me that's not very healthy." She meandered to the coffee pot and poured a fresh cup. "Cream or sugar?"

"Um, sugar. Four spoons."

"Brave man."

He eased into a chair at the kitchen table. "How does this amnesia thing work? You remember how to make coffee."

"I remember how to do a lot of things. I know what things are called, I know how to function. Just can't remember anything before the hospital."

"Except your name," he said, accepting the coffee mug from her.

She pulled out the chair next to him and sat down. "Yes, my name. There are a few other things, but they're…" She propped her elbow on the table, and her fingers curled against her mouth.

"They're what?"

"I don't know how to explain it." Her hand dropped from her mouth. "Surreal? Like they're dream fragments coming back to me, but I can't quite grasp them all. The ones I do hold onto are… crazy." She laughed to herself. "There's that word again."

"You're not crazy." He lifted the mug to his lips, and a stale taste overwhelmed his taste buds. He forced the liquid down his throat. "And, that is the absolute worst coffee I've ever had."

Kaylen's forehead crinkled as she sampled the coffee in her own mug. "Oh, that's horrible!"

"Where'd you get that from?"

"It was in the back of the pantry, third shelf down."

"I didn't even know I had it." He grimaced, but a smile played on his lips. "Probably expired back in the nineties."

"Now I know why you go to the diner so much."

"We'll grab some breakfast there before I leave you with Hannah for the day. Get some real coffee, too."

"Can I just follow you for the day? A police ride-along?"

"Sure. I'll just deputize you for the day."

"Really?"

"No, not really." His smile turned into a contagious laugh that infected her as well.

"Fine, fine. But, I can ride with you, right?" Her lips curved down, and she picked at her fingernails. "Not that Hannah isn't great, but with everything that's happened, I'd feel safer with you."

He'd had the same thoughts, but wasn't sure she would want to stick with him. Hannah would at least keep her mind occupied, while he would do nothing but paperwork and head out on the occasional call. "Yeah, you can come with me. I can't guarantee any level of excitement, though."

"That's fine," she said.

Her hands thudded against the table, and her tattoos once again caught his attention. He leaned over, lifted her arm, and turned it over to look at the black ink. Realizing he had just invaded her space, he let go of her. "I'm sorry."

"It's okay. I look at them all the time, wondering what they are."

"They're symbols, I think."

Her palm ran back and forth over her arm as if she were trying to warm it up. "I think you're right. I just wish I knew what they meant."

"You think they mean something, too?"

"I can't see me getting a bunch of random tattoos that don't mean anything. But, why so many?"

He let go of her arm, but continued staring at it. "They're evenly spaced out. Like they're specifically placed."

"I thought that, too. Doesn't help with the meaning, though."

"Maybe we can take a picture of some of them and see what we can find." Leaning back in his chair, he asked, "Have you remembered anything else?"

"This morning, when I woke from a weird dream. At least I thought it was a dream, but when I woke up, I realized it was more of a memory." She fidgeted, and her hand flew up to her mouth. Nibbling at the edges of a fingernail, her shoulders heaved with a large sigh.

"Do you want to tell me about it?"

"I thought it was a dream. There were these people around me, looking down at me. Four or five, I think. Except they had no faces. Just black holes where their eyes should have been. The rest of their skin was stretched over where their noses and mouths were."

A chill ran through his body, encasing his veins in ice. "Did they say anything?"

"Yeah, but it was something foreign. I tried to identify it, but I couldn't recognize it as a language. They all seemed to understand it, though, 'cause they had a full conversation."

"Are you sure it wasn't a dream?"

"It felt much too real. I can recall every detail. The strange thing is that I know them. I know who they are, I just can't remember."

He rolled the images around in his mind. "I'm not a psychologist or anything, but maybe the strange faces were there to conceal their identity since you lost your memory. Your mind created them because it had to see something."

"I don't think so." She gulped in air as if her lungs were starved for it, then blew it out. "I've seen those faces before. Everything about them was familiar. The way the stretched-out skin wrinkled around the nose, the flatness where a mouth should be, the gaping eye sockets. I've seen it all before."

"That's... that's impossible."

"I know. But, it's true."

The seriousness of her tone and pleading eyes convinced him

of that. She had said that her memories left her with a bit of lunacy, and he couldn't argue. Horrific faces, nonexistent foreign languages...

"They knew me, too," she continued, tears brimming at her eyelids. "At least, I think they did. They were talking to me, but not *to me*. Like they were talking right through me."

Peter didn't quite grasp her meaning, but her fear was all-too real. She wasn't telling him just to let him know, but so that someone would reassure her of her sanity. The last two days had taught him that his wildest nightmares were no longer so far-fetched.

His hand covered hers, and he gave a slight squeeze. "I believe you."

She stared at him for a moment, tears receding before they spilled over. Her breath came out in an airy laugh. "Thank goodness, because I don't think I believe it myself."

"It's okay," he said, letting go of her hand. "I can't imagine how you feel, but you're telling the truth about what you've remembered. Is there anything else?"

She shook her head. "I don't know if I want anything else to come back to me."

"It'll come. How are the headaches?"

Her gaze flicked away from him. "Fine." She popped up out of the kitchen chair. "Ready to go? I'm starving."

Watching her leave the kitchen, he slowly rose from his chair, convinced she was lying about the headaches. Yet, she had been so forthcoming about the strange memories. There was no reason to lie about anything else. He decided to press her about it later, when she wasn't so emotionally raw. For now, he'd accept what she said and pray she wasn't lying about anything else.

Chapter Fourteen

S tomachs filled with a homespun breakfast from the diner, Peter and Kaylen sat opposite each other at his desk at the station. Shirley found their visitor a chair and served up a cup of warm coffee. Although they enjoyed a steaming mug at the diner, the gray chilled the air almost as much as the boundless depths of winter. That kind of chill – the one that reached deep inside and fused itself with Peter's bones – could only be exterminated with hot drink or a long, steaming shower. Until then, shivers would rattle his interior, if not the whole of his body.

Upon leaving the diner, Peter had expected to see butterflies again. The slight variations in the air, the life he once lived fading into the distance, taunted him. He almost needed to see the flight of the colorful creatures to bring him hope. But, as he stared out the window of his office, the sky only held dark, threatening clouds. The gray would be gone in another week or so, but until then, the rain would pummel the town. He feared they had yet to experience the worst of it.

Kaylen clapped her hands together, rousing Peter to the present. "What to do first?"

He cleared his throat and shuffled a few papers on his desk. Financial reports for the mayor, budget requests, supply and reimbursement requisites. All the mundane things of the world that seemed to matter less each day that Kaylen stayed in town.

"Since things are quiet this morning," he said, once the papers were stacked to the side, "we'll look further into your tattoos."

"In other words, we have nothing to go on."

"Not necessarily," he said, a bit of exaggeration in his tone. His eyes landed on her tattoos, and he held his hand out. "May I?"

"Oh, of course." Hands stretched toward him, she laid her forearms on the desk.

He traced the curve of one of the tattoos with his index and middle fingers. They followed the half-circle into the downward slant and to where it abruptly ended in another half-circle. "These symbols." His thumb brushed over a second one, a triangle this time, interlocked with three circles. "They aren't random. They mean *something*. There has to be some information we can find online."

"What if we can't find anything?"

"I suppose we could drive out to the university in Wichita. See if there's a professor there who knows anything about..." He glanced down at the black symbols on her arm. "Well, whatever culture these come from. You know, I'm no tattoo expert, but these look new. There's no fading. Crisp, clean, like they were done last week. And, this many tattoos would take a long time and cost a lot of money."

"Following that logic," she said, "even if it's been a few months since I got them, someone would remember them and me."

He turned to his computer. "We could call tattoo shops. Find out if you got them around here." He pulled up a list of local tattoo parlors within a 100-mile radius. "Lots of them in Wichita to contact, but not much outside of that. One over in Derby. Two in Hutchinson."

"Sounds like a great place to start. Hopefully I paid with a credit card."

A couple hours later, he replaced the phone in the cradle, having struck out with the last shop. "Nothing."

"I left messages at several shops," Kaylen said. "Everyone else said they don't remember me."

Peter absorbed her downtrodden expression and slumped shoulders. "We'll figure this out." Taking his cell phone out of his pocket, he navigated the touch screen to his camera. "Some tattoo shops post pictures of their work online, so I'm going to take pictures of the tattoos and upload them. See if we can track them that way. If anything, we might find a match for some of the symbols and learn what they mean."

She laid her arm on the desk, and Peter adjusted the camera's zoom until he had one symbol in frame. He pressed the round circle at the bottom of the phone to take the picture, but nothing happened. His finger stabbed at the button, two, three, four times. Still, nothing.

He shook the phone. Random colors streaked the screen, disappearing when he held it still. Hovering the phone over her arm again, he tried several more times to take the photo, but his phone continued to malfunction.

"What's wrong?" Kaylen asked.

"Can't seem to get the camera to work." He pressed the power button to turn off the phone, hoping a quick reboot would solve the issue.

"Sheriff?" Shirley's voice called over the intercom.

"Yes?"

"Wyatt Whitaker is on the line. Says you need to go out there. He's having a fit. Something to do with his livestock."

Peter rubbed his temples. He thought Wyatt would be taken care of for a while with Keith in the psych hospital in Wichita. "Let him know I'm heading out." He glanced at Kaylen. "Do you want to stay here or go with me?"

"With you," she said, already standing up. She stretched her arms over her head. "Livestock has to be more exciting than calling tattoo parlors."

A smile took over his face, and his eyebrows shot up. "Always."

They walked back through the back of the station toward the parking lot. One of the most important clues he had to Kaylen's identity sparked in his mind, something he had overlooked with everything that had happened in the past two days. "Give me just a minute."

He left Kaylen and jogged to the front of the station to Shirley's desk in the lobby. He snatched her legal pad and a pen off her desk. After jotting down Kaylen's license plate number from memory, he slid the pad back toward Shirley. "Can you run that plate for me?"

"Sure." She scribbled her own indecipherable notes underneath it. "How fast do you need it?"

"If you could get it today for me. I've neglected it long enough."

Shirley stared up at him, eyes squinted, lips pressed into a thin line.

"Did you have something else?" he asked.

"Are you okay? I know a lot has happened, and we're all tore up about Fred and Belinda, but even before that, you weren't acting quite yourself."

He paused a long moment to let go of the stress and heartache and mystery that had devoured his mundane life. Could his demeanor have changed from the time he learned about Kaylen's accident? If so, he wouldn't have realized it. No time to analyze his own behavior. He'd barely acknowledged Fred's death. A few moments before his eyes closed the night before, and a furtive, bereaved glance with Hannah that morning in the diner were the only times his friend's death started to penetrate his core. Other than that, he hadn't slowed down a bit to consider any effect the events may have had on him.

Then again, he'd always struggled with the concept of grief. One day, he'd have to give himself over to mourning Fred, Belinda, and their baby, allow the tears and the pain to come. He wouldn't hold it back this time, wouldn't allow a cesspool of sorrow to fester inside. Not like he did with his mom's death.

Just as he was about to respond to Shirley, movement outside the window caught his attention. "What the hell?"

"Peter!" Kaylen ran into the lobby. She stopped when she reached him, her gaze stuck on the street in the front of the station. "They're in the back, too."

He stepped toward the window cautiously, as if he moved too fast, they would see him and attack. A kaleidoscope, made up of what seemed like hundreds of butterflies, hovered over Main Street. Flapping wings littered the sky above the asphalt, a living child's coloring book with swirls of abstract colors crossing over the lines.

Until now, the appearance of the butterflies seemed random. But, a connection formed in his mind, one that terrified him. He first saw the flying insects with the discovery of Kaylen's accident and amnesia. Then, came Fred's house when they discovered the bodies. The inn, before the attempted break-in. There had hardly been an incident in the past few days without the butterflies first announcing it.

He swiveled to face Shirley, who had joined them at the window. "When did Wyatt Whitaker call about the livestock?"

Her eyes fixated on the scene outside, she said, "Just now,

when I told you."

"What did he say, exactly?"

"Just that he was upset about his livestock, but he didn't make much sense." Turning to Peter, she asked, "Sheriff, what's going on here?"

Instead of responding, he signaled Kaylen, who nodded at his unspoken words. "I'll check in from Wyatt's," he said to Shirley. "Call Ollie and have him meet me out there."

He heard Kaylen matching his hurried steps behind him as he raced through the station toward the back lot.

Chapter Fifteen

B lood.
  Everywhere he looked, Peter saw blood. Crimson and coagulated, smeared across the ground like an artist with an out-of-control paintbrush. Grass, muddy patches, all textured with innards and unspeakable matter. The sickening scent of decay swelled in the morning breeze. The sulfuric odor, rotten eggs mixed with garlic, turning it into something indescribable, swirled around Peter's nostrils. It penetrated his pores and seeped into the fabric of his uniform. Nature had forsaken the earth and air, giving it over to the only inevitable part of life: death.

Then, there were the bodies.

Dairy cows, once plump and ready for milking, once alive and grazing happily. These cows looked nothing like those others, the ones they had been before... before *this*. But, Peter couldn't quite figure out what *this* was.

"He did it." Wyatt stood opposite of Peter and Ollie. Between them laid four cows from his deceased herd, eighty-two cows in total. Wyatt had worked hard and was proud of his herd; his kids even had names for their favorites.

Peter had to shout for Wyatt to hear him across the wide span of carnage. "Keith didn't do it. He's locked up in a psych ward in Wichita." Upon Wyatt's first accusation that Keith Dusky had murdered his cows in an act of revenge, Peter had called the psychiatric hospital just to be sure. Even though the Keith he knew would never dream of hurting Wyatt's livestock, the man he arrested a few days earlier certainly might be capable of such a thing.

"Then he sent someone to do it." Wyatt walked around the

cattle, his eyes examining the bloodshed.

"How did he do that?" Ollie asked. "He has no phone privileges."

"I don't know, but these heifers were fine this morning. Tanya and I dropped the kids at school, then went to the feed store out in El Dorado. Come back an hour later to find this. How can someone do this in broad daylight in an hour?"

How, indeed? Peter wondered. It would take several people to kill this many cows in that short of a timespan. But why didn't the animals charge their attackers or even run from the danger? Kansas history was littered with cases of cattle mutilation, but there was usually no blood left at the scenes, causing UFO enthusiasts to blame otherworldly creatures. This case, however, contained as much blood as if the skies had opened and rained it down.

Peter caught sight of the desperation on Wyatt's face. His dairy cows were a large part of his livelihood. Most farmers in the area barely scraped by with their income. It would be near impossible to replace the herd.

"Let's go on inside," Wyatt said. "I can't keep looking at this."

"I'm gonna grab my camera out of the car," Ollie said. "I'll get some pictures and then make those calls to gather some help out here to clean it up." He jogged in the direction of his patrol car.

"Do the kids have a friend they can stay with tonight in case it's not done?" Peter asked.

"Yeah, yeah," Wyatt said as he started walking toward the house. "I'll have Tanya set it up."

"I'm going to call that wildlife expert from Kansas State University," Peter said. "The one who came down when the Higgins' chickens started dying a couple years' back. Maybe he can help figure out how the cattle died."

"I'd say having their intestines chopped up and dragged out of 'em did the trick," Wyatt said.

Peter bristled. He couldn't blame Wyatt for his sarcasm, but he could also do without it and the descriptive terms that resurrected the images in his mind. "Let's just get the right people out here to help. Tanya hasn't seen it, has she?"

"'Course not. I told 'er, but you'd think it was just another day on the farm," Wyatt said, throwing up his hands. "Woman's been baking all day like she's feeding the whole county."

"Baking?" Peter asked. It seemed an odd reaction to the news that their entire herd had died.

"Dunno what's gotten into her," Wyatt said, opening the screen door on the back of their farmhouse.

The aroma of vanilla extract assaulted Peter as if he had sniffed it straight from a bottle, but mixed with the unmistakable scent of freshly baked bread, it caused his mouth to water. He followed Wyatt around the corner into the kitchen and saw that there was no exaggeration about Tanya's baking spree. Loaves of bread were stacked on the counter, a tower so tall it leaned against the refrigerator for support. A mess of cookies spanned the counter, bridged across the stove, and onto the opposite countertop, as if Tanya had just thrown them on top of each other after pulling them out of the oven. Peter saw a hint of aluminum foil underneath it all, protecting the base of the cookies from any unwanted debris on the counter. As his eyes scanned the treats, he recognized everything from snickerdoodles, to macaroons, to old-fashioned chocolate chip, all mingling together without any hint of organization.

His gaze landed on Tanya, who furiously whipped at some mix in a metal bowl. Between the dings of her wire whisk hitting the edges of the bowl, his ears picked up on her mumbling. He inched closer to her, his head turned so he could hear better, but he still couldn't make out what she said.

"Hey, Tanya," he said. "Is there a church bake sale coming up?"

She whirled around, her whisking hand not missing a beat. "Brownies! They love brownies."

Peter peeked into the bowl, the telltale brown mixture spinning over and through her whisk. "Brownies are great."

"Biscuits," she continued, as if Peter hadn't spoken. "They always loved my biscuits. And, cornbread! Must have cornbread!" She turned back to the counter, lifted her mixing bowl, and brownie batter cascaded in ribbons into an oiled glass dish.

He didn't notice Kaylen until she stepped up beside him. Arms folded, she stared at Tanya's back. Wrinkles formed around concerned eyes as she glanced at Peter. She shook her head, a silent gesture that said so much.

"Ready?" he asked, his voice quiet so as not to disturb Tanya's trance.

Kaylen started toward the foyer, and Peter followed, nodding for Wyatt to join them. When they reached the front porch, he grimaced and tried to figure out how to broach Tanya's odd behavior.

"Has this ever happened before?" Kaylen asked.

Though her question surprised Peter, he was grateful for her opening the conversation.

"She's been like this all mornin'," Wyatt said. "Maybe she's upset about the cows. She gets busy when she's stressed."

"Do you want me to call Doc Horton?" Peter asked. "Maybe he can stop by and see—"

"Nah," Wyatt said. "I'm sure once the cows are cleared out she'll be fine." He slapped Peter's back. "Thanks for comin' out."

"I'll update you when I have a report on the official cause of death," Peter said.

Kaylen thrust her hand at Wyatt, who accepted it in a firm shake. "Nice to meet you," she said.

"You, too." He nodded at them both. "Good day, Sheriff."

They parted ways, and Peter walked with Kaylen toward his patrol car. Once they were out of earshot, Peter said, "I'm sorry you had to witness that."

"Does she... is she manic?" Kaylen asked.

"Not a day since I've known her."

"Hmm."

"Why do you ask?"

"I've seen it before."

Peter halted at her nonchalant tone. He grabbed her arm to stop her walking. "What? What do you mean you've seen it before?"

She stepped back and shook her arm from his hand. "I just mean..." Her shoulders heaved with a deep breath, and her tongue darted across her lips. "It's hard to explain."

"Try."

"Before you came inside, I was watching her. She never once stopped moving, barely stopped talking. That's when the images came. Just flashes of faces and movements. I know I've seen other people like her." Kaylen's forehead creased, and her lips curved down. "*Exactly* like her."

He wanted to respond, but couldn't form the words. His gut writhed with dread, an all-too-familiar feeling the past few days.

"What happened to the livestock?" Kaylen asked.

"I don't think—"

"No, I need to know. I don't know why, but I need to."

After hesitating, he told Kaylen of the carnage on Wyatt's farm as they continued to his car. He balked at the details, but she insisted, so he relayed everything. With every sentence, he could almost see her memory returning… the spark behind her eyes, the twitch of her lips.

When they reached the car, he stopped her again before getting in. "What does all this have to do with you?"

She flinched, but recovered from her initial shock. "I don't know. A lot of bad things have happened here lately, haven't they? And, it's only started recently?"

"Since you came to town." He hated being honest about it, but it seemed more and more that she was directly related to the strange events. "What are you remembering?"

"Random things. Strings of memories that really don't make sense. Except they do make sense. Then there's this damned…" Her face scrunched up, and she reached for the side of her head. "Please, let's just go."

"I think I should take you to the clinic so the doc can have a look at you."

"I don't want—"

"I don't care," he said. "You're going."

She challenged him with her eyes for a moment, but relented and nodded. Without a word, she climbed into the car.

Peter waited for a moment, to catch his breath and slow his thoughts. A thick raindrop landed on his forehead and rolled down his face. His head lulled back, and he glanced up at the sky, into the foreboding gray.

Chapter Sixteen

As the sun descended over the town, filling the sky with brilliant hues of pink, blue, and orange, Peter and Kaylen found Doc Horton in the lobby of the clinic. "How's my favorite patient?" he asked Kaylen.

Peter chuckled at the question, one he was sure the doctor asked several times a day.

"I'm doing well, thank you," Kaylen said, her head down and a slight blush filling her cheeks as she reverted back into her timid state. "I hate wasting your time—"

"You can stop with that nonsense now," the doctor said, humor in his tone. "I wanted to see you tomorrow anyway for a checkup, so I'm glad the sheriff called. I'm just sorry to have to see you so late in the day, but Lou Ann isn't here, so it's been a little busy."

"She sick?" Peter asked. To his knowledge, Lou Ann never took time off.

"Not sure," Doc Horton said. "She left for a late lunch, but hasn't come back. I've called a couple times, but hadn't been able to check in on her yet. Too busy here. She said she wasn't feeling well earlier so I'm sure she's fine, but do you mind running by her place?"

"Sure thing," Peter said. "What time should I come back?"

"We'll be a few hours," Doc Horton said. "I want to run some tests and make sure everything is healing up fine."

"Just call when she's ready." Peter turned to Kaylen. "You okay here without me?"

"I'll be fine," she said.

Peter waved goodbye and headed back to his car. Lou Ann's

home wasn't too far away, only three miles. Within minutes, he pulled into the driveway and walked up the front steps. He rang the doorbell. When it failed to chime, he rapped three times on the screen door. He paced in front of the "Welcome" mat until he heard the front door creak open.

"Sheriff." Lou Ann's voice came from behind the dark screen door. The sun hit the house from the perfect direction to shade her form and face. "What can I do for ya?"

"Hey, Lou Ann. Was just over at the clinic. Doc Horton was a bit worried since you didn't come back from lunch. Asked me to come check on you."

"Just a bit under the weather, that's all."

"Seems to be going 'round," Peter said. "You need a ride over to see the doc?"

"I'm fine." Her fist covered her mouth as a forced cough emerged.

Before Peter could say anything else, the door slammed shut. Stunned, he raised his hand to knock again, but quickly lowered it. Shaking off the encounter, he retraced his steps back to his patrol car, considering that, yet again, another resident of Nowhere was acting out of character. Lou Ann's golden heart and warm disposition had driven her distinguished, lifelong career as a nurse. Peter could attest to her gracious bedside manner; she had cared for him in his younger years, whenever he had a seizure. He'd never seen her cross with anyone, let alone outright dismissive.

Once settled in the driver's seat of his car, he pushed the key into the ignition, then looked up at Lou Ann's house. It seemed his whole town had entered another dimension. In Nowhere's history, there'd only been one murder, back in 1925. Though the state of Kansas had experienced cattle mutilations, more than most states, not one had occurred in Nowhere. Even then, those other incidents included a bloodless scene. The one at Wyatt's farm did not technically fall under the classification of mutilation; it was a massacre. As for Kaylen's accident, he didn't know the stats on hit and runs, but he knew there hadn't been one since before he moved to town.

But, in the past three days, all of these things – and more – had occurred under his watch. Peter wondered what would happen if this... whatever it was... took hold of more people. His station was well-stocked with deputies, but he didn't know if they would be enough, especially should the strange illness afflict one of them. Thankfully, there was no indication that these strange occurrences would continue. The town could very well be on the tail end of a bad luck spree.

He dropped his face into his hands, his fingertips massaging his forehead. Banging on the passenger window made him jump. Lou Ann frantically slammed her palms against the passenger's side window until he lowered it.

"Peter," she said, "I need help."

Spurred on by the urgency in her voice, he unbuckled his seatbelt and hopped out of the car. He raced around to the other side. "What's going on?"

Terror filled her eyes and pinched her brow. "I don't know. Something's not right. I don't feel…"

He waited a moment for her to finish, but she didn't. "You don't feel what?"

A shadow crossed her face and settled into her eyes, turning the hazel two shades darker. Her expression cleared up, and her lips thinned. "Nothing, Sheriff. I've just been a bit under the weather. I'm sorry to bother you." She whipped around and started back toward her house.

"Lou Ann!"

She turned around and said, "Be sober, be vigilant; because your adversary the devil, as a roaring lion, walketh about, seeking whom he may devour." As soon as the last word of the Bible verse left her mouth, she continued her trek back to her house.

"Lou Ann! Wait!"

She didn't stop, only continued into her house and slammed the front door shut. The screen door she left ajar squeaked as the breeze wobbled it back and forth.

His hand snaked around the back of his neck, rubbing at the tense muscles. He could have gone after her, pressed her for more information, but he didn't. As the sheriff, he had no legal reason to compel her to tell him anything. She wasn't in danger, at least as far as he could tell, and she insisted she was ill. Her actions could be blamed on a fever, he supposed, but he doubted it.

Peter climbed back into his car and drove away, debating if he should call Doc Horton to make a house call. He decided to talk to the doctor when he picked up Kaylen from the clinic. As long as Lou Ann didn't shoot someone, she could wait a little longer.

Chapter Seventeen

Driving back to the station, Peter spied Hannah's pickup truck at the park, and he decided to stop. Sadness washed over him at the sight, knowing she was there for one reason: to sort through the avalanche of emotions that came with mourning.

The park – aptly called Middle Park – was located in the middle of the town. Outsiders often kidded about the Middle Park of Nowhere, not realizing the locals had heard every possible joke about their town. Peter had grown up playing on the equipment after school with Hannah. As they grew older, they reserved the swings for more serious talks. He knew Hannah tended to retreat there to clear her thoughts, often times calling Peter to join her. As he approached the swings, he briefly wondered why she hadn't reached out to him tonight.

"Petey Holbrook."

Peter smiled at the familiar nickname called out by his favorite voice. The feigned anger in his eyes contradicted the smirk on his lips. "If we're pulling out the oldies, I have a few nicknames in my pocket from your childhood, too."

Hannah laughed. Jerking the chain of the swing next to her, an invite for him to join her, she said, "It seems we're searching for the same thing tonight." Her gaze traveled the length of the chain, to the top of the swing set. "That elusive clarity."

Peter settled into the swing next to her and stared ahead, contemplating her words. He supposed that while she was correct in some regards, the act of coming here couldn't be as easily explained as that. He did not know what he sought tonight. Possibly a return to the simpler days, when his only concerns involved epilepsy, math tests, and his pesky crush on Hannah.

Kicking her legs into the air, Hannah started the motion of the swing, continuing until she attained a bit of height, but not too much.

He rocked back and forth on his own swing until he caught up to her. Far from being in sync, his swing wobbled a bit, much as it did in their school days when they sat side-by-side. Their swings lost momentum as they talked and laughed through their favorite childhood memories.

When the swings slowed, Hannah twisted side to side in hers. "Perfect world?" she asked, her eyes staring out into the clouded night.

"Oh no," Peter said.

"Come on," she said. "Perfect world?"

A game they played as children and into their teens, and only on the swings on which they sat, they would take turns stating all the things that they believed would make their worlds perfect at that moment. Though their lists always changed with time – Peter being awarded a baseball scholarship to Wichita State University, Hannah having her own horse, and so on – they were always truthful, minus one thing. Peter never let on that his perfect world would always have Hannah in it.

That wish hadn't wavered once over the years, though there were times when he admitted it wasn't likely to come true, at least not in the way he desired. She would always stand beside him as a friend, but nothing more.

Tonight's list was sure to be grim, so Peter didn't hold back. "Okay, perfect world. Fred and Belinda back."

"With their baby," Hannah added. "A perfect little girl."

"What were they going to name her again?"

"Denise." She slowed her swing, dust kicking up around her feet as they dragged.

"Denise. We don't have one of those around here."

"Sure don't." She sniffled. "I don't… I don't understand why. Why would Belinda do that? She loved him so… so much." Her chest heaved, and she emitted a restrained, breathy cry.

Peter turned his swing and placed a hand on her forearm, chastising himself for not doing more. A stronger man would take her in his arms and provide the comfort and security for which she longed. A stronger man would do everything he could to win her heart. A stronger man…

Someone other than him. He was more like the Cowardly Lion when it came to love. He would rather wait for it to happen to him rather than take control of the situation, forcing their relationship to the next level. The level he thought they both wanted. But, what if he was wrong about that? The one looming question that always stopped him short.

Hannah wiped her silent tears with her shirt sleeve and laughed. "I'm such a wimp when it comes to these things."

"You're not," he said, hoping to reassure her. "It's a horrible thing, and no one is expected to be strong when it comes to losing two of your closest friends."

"What's happening to our town, Peter?"

"I'm not sure," he said, the words making him wonder if he should have been that honest with her. But, her question made him think she wasn't just speaking about Fred and Belinda. "Have you noticed anything else strange around town?" he asked.

"Actually, yeah. Lyle Shepard came into the diner today. Asked for a whole pecan pie."

"He what?" Everyone in town knew Lyle had a severe nut allergy, one that could kill him. He made sure to tell anyone he came across, even those who already knew.

"I didn't give it to him, of course. I thought he was joking at first, but he became angry when I refused to sell it to him. Carlos ran him out."

"Why would Lyle ask for a pecan pie?"

"You got me."

Peter's cell phone rang, startling him. He pulled it out of his pocket and saw it was Doc Horton. "Hey, Doc," he said when he answered.

"Sheriff. Kaylen's ready for you. Didn't take nearly as long as we planned."

Rising from the swing, Peter said, "I'll be there in a few minutes." He ended the call and placed his phone back in his pocket. "I have to head back to the clinic to get Kaylen."

Hannah slipped off her swing. "Is she doing better? Any memories coming back?"

"A few here and there, I think. But, she seems to be doing well other than that." His eyes searched Hannah's still-saddened expression. "I'm sorry you have to go through this with Fred and Belinda."

"Yeah, same to you. I'm sorry any of us have to do it."

"Better days are coming, I promise you."

"They are, are they?" She let out a small giggle. "Do you remember when you asked me to marry you?"

A smile crossed Peter's lips. "That doesn't sound like me."

She swatted the back of her hand against his upper arm.

"Ow!" he said, laughing.

"You know damn well you did. We were in seventh grade—"

"Fifth grade," Peter corrected.

"Sixth grade it was," she said. "Right here, in front of these swings, after the last day of school, you got on your knees and asked me to marry you." She wandered onto the grass, her back toward him. "Do you remember my answer?"

"How can I forget?" His eyes bored into the back of her red hair. "You said, 'Not even if you were sheriff.'"

She turned around and shared a melancholic laugh with him. "Maybe you should ask me again."

"So, what?" He waved his hands around the empty playground. "You can humiliate me again in front of all our friends?"

"You never know what answer you might get, Sheriff."

Peter's curiosity overrode his sensibility, and he walked over to her. He knew she expected him to stop a couple feet in front of her, so he continued toward her until they were inches apart. He smiled down at her surprised expression and, though entirely tempted to kiss her after all the years of inaction, he lowered himself down until his knee sunk into the sand.

Hannah stepped back and watched him with unreadable eyes.

He wanted to reach for her hand, but held back the urge. "Hannah Katherine O'Brien, will you marry me?"

Her breath shuddered in the night air, but she quickly composed herself with a playful expression. Moving backward, slowly, away from him, she said, "I need to think about it."

Peter flinched, not expecting that answer. "Think about it?" He lifted his hands up and shrugged. "You're actually gonna leave me hanging like this? Leave a guy on his knees, begging?"

"Sorry, Sheriff. Big decision, and I have to open the diner in the morning." She winked at him. "Ask again later."

He shrugged out his arms. "I could have gotten that answer from a Magic-8 Ball."

Instead of answering, she waved goodbye. He waited for

Hannah to disappear around the corner before getting to his feet, just as he had in the fifth, sixth, or seventh grade, minus the embarrassment. He had played this game long enough with her to know that there may never be a resolution. For now, he'd have to be okay with that.

His phone rang again, but Shirley's name popped up on the screen. "Hey, Shirley. What can for ya?"

"Sorry so late, Sheriff, but I just got those plates run on the girl's car."

His heart thumped in his chest at the possible answer to her identity. "You got a name?"

"Sure do, but it ain't no woman's name."

He paused as the information sunk in. "Say again?"

"Some guy named Walter Guthrie owns the car those plates belong to."

His gut churned. "Did he let someone borrow it?" he asked out of desperation.

"Nope. Plates were stolen a few months back."

"Okay," he said, taking a deep breath. "Thanks for letting me know." His mind raced with the possibilities. Kaylen was a criminal, obviously, since she had stolen the plates. So, what else had she done that she couldn't remember?

But, then again, he didn't know for sure she had stolen them. There might be a good explanation for it all, even though he might not know it until her memory returned in full.

"Shirley? Do me a favor and keep this between us. No need to let the rest of the deputies or anyone else know."

"You got it, Sheriff. Have a good night."

"You, too." Entangled in questions, he jogged to his car. One thing he did know, was that even if she stole those plates, someone had run her off the road and later tried to break into her hotel room. The girl was still in danger, no matter who she turned out to be.

Chapter Eighteen

I must be crazy.

The thought crossed Peter's mind over and over, but it didn't stop him from driving Kaylen back to his house after he picked her up at the clinic. Upon discovering the plates on her car – and quite possibly the car itself – were stolen, he should have taken her to the station and into custody.

But, he never once let on about the stolen plates. In fact, he decided to ignore the lawbreaking altogether until her memory returned. At that time, he could at least properly interrogate her and determine the extent of the crime committed.

He knew he was talking himself into seeing her as a victim over criminal, that he was purposely ignoring the law to keep her in his care, but somehow, it seemed the best option for the situation. He just hoped he didn't later regret it.

After they reached his home, they each retreated into their rooms, exhausted from the day. He fell asleep almost the moment his head hit the pillow and lost himself in a flurry of odd, disjointed dreams.

Sometime in the middle of the night, Peter's eyes flicked open, as if someone had called his name and shook him awake. He focused on the darkness outside his balcony doors, wishing he had closed the blinds before retiring for the night. The wind whipped through the large oak tree in the middle of his yard and, beyond that, the pine and oak trees bordering his property.

Yet, it wasn't just the wind that moved.

He slipped the covers off his chilled body and swung his feet over the edge of the bed. Easing himself off, his limbs moved on their own accord, summoned toward the darkness. When he reached the doors, he rested his hands on the pane of glass that separated him from the gray. His eyes adjusted to the night, and colors appeared in the dark green of the oak. Wings, thousands of them, fluttered in the wind, rustling the leaves more than any spring thunderstorm. The sight of the butterflies sucked the breath from his chest, stealing his life force little by little, until the blood in his face stopped flowing.

The door opened behind him, and his lungs seemed to operate once more. He didn't turn around, but waited until Kaylen crept up beside him to speak.

"You feel it, too," he said.

"Yes." Her shallow breaths mirrored the fear growing inside of him.

"What is it?"

She didn't respond, but she didn't have to. He knew, they both knew, the gray housed something dreadful that they would both soon face. The two strangers, one of whom only knew her name, would throw themselves into the dark to face an unidentifiable evil. Whatever lurked out there, perhaps the best possible outcome for them both was death.

Her hand slipped into his, stemming the horrific thoughts looming over the gray in his mind. An unexplainable peace flowed into him, relieving his tense muscles, and almost guiding him back to sleep. Kaylen also seemed to relax beside him, as her breathing slowed and evened out. What was it about this woman? Why – *how* – did she have this effect over him?

Peter started to speak the question aloud when something caught his attention outside the doors. He focused his eyes toward the movement. A single butterfly had broken away from the swarm and found its way to his balcony. It landed on the window in front of him. The colors aroused a memory of the morning at the diner when he first heard about Kaylen. The butterfly had touched his nose that day and now it sat in front of him, fluttering its wings to get his attention, yet not taking flight. His mind spoke to him of impossibility and improbability, made calculations of the statistics on this being the same butterfly. But, it was the same. His soul told him that and, in that moment, it spoke much louder than any rational part of his brain.

His butterfly.

Peter's muscles tensed again, like the end of a kid's slingshot, ready to fire. His eyes widened as he watched the butterfly's wings move without lifting it away from the glass. Was it trying to speak? Tell him something in nature's Morse Code?

His mouth moved without thought. "It's the door. It's opened."

Her head snapped toward him. "What? What did you say?"

"The do—"

He stopped speaking, unable to complete his thought.

"Peter? What about the door?"

Kaylen's voice washed over him, but he could not force his mind to answer her or even focus on her face that floated in front of him.

"Peter!"

Her panicked sound did not rouse him from his state. A vile odor filtered into his nostrils, one he couldn't immediately place. Rotting food, rotten eggs... decay. No, not decay. Something much worse. The smell of the malevolence living inside the gray.

Death.

Chapter Nineteen

*P*eter drifted through the mist-filled hallways, almost as if his feet did not touch the ground. More like floating rather than walking, which heightened his anxiety.

He stopped when he reached a circular room, a cul-de-sac of sorts, and he turned just in time to see the pathway behind him disappear. Two doors with arches overhead materialized on either side of the room, the wood curving to the bend with the white walls. Though structurally impossible, there they stood, with thick, stale air surrounding them, as if waiting for him to make a choice. Which door to enter? Which one would result in life and which in death?

He waited for many moments, though he could not tell how long. Time seemed not to matter in the room. He could have spent a hundred years in there already, or maybe it was only a hundred seconds. His gaze shifted from door to door, but he dared not open either for fear of making the wrong decision. Instead, he sat on the cold, white marble floor, facing in a direction where he could not see either door. The starkness of the white hurt his eyes, tunneling his sight with brightness all around.

One of the doors shifted into his peripheral vision, and he realized the room had started moving. Slowly, but not for long. The floor seemed to stay in the same place, but the walls rotated, faster, then faster still, until the doors melded and blurred into one. The absence of sound prickled his nerves until he covered his ears, afraid of what might happen if something made a noise. He sealed his eyes shut. He couldn't stay in this room much longer, not with the torturous spinning and lack of sound.

"Peter."

The angelic voice penetrated his defenses. One eyelid cracked open to see if it was safe. The room had stopped its insane movement, and he opened his eyes all the way.

"I'm right here, Peter."

He glanced over his shoulder. A woman stood behind him, but he didn't recognize her until he rose to a standing position and turned around.

"Mom?"

Her smile was just as he remembered it. So caring, so nurturing, so pure in its love for him. Just like a mother should smile at her child. Her shoulder-length brunette hair caught in a breeze, as if a light fan blew on her. The blue eyes he remembered as a child shone brighter than any star. Peter was more distracted by the soft aura around her, however, the only attribute that had changed from her days on Earth.

"How are you here?" he asked. "Am I dead?"

"No, Peter. It's not your time."

"Where… where are we?"

"The In Between."

As soon as she spoke the words, he knew them to be true. He was caught between life and death – the two doors. His mind roamed to the last thing he remembered, and he recalled the strange odors and the inability to speak before his world went black. "Did I have a seizure?"

"You did, and you have yet to wake up from it."

He shook his head. "You can't be here. You're in Heaven. I must be dreaming."

"This is no dream, and we don't have long before you're called back. Something is coming, Peter. Something is coming to Nowhere, and it's searching you out. It may already be there."

Dread thickened his blood. "What is it?"

"Something you've been preparing for your whole life. You'll need every ability you possess to fight it. To keep yourself safe. To keep the girl safe."

"Kaylen?" Her name rolled off his lips and hung in the air between them. "Who is she? What is she doing in Nowhere?"

"You have seen things, Peter," she said, not answering his question. "Things you have blocked out from your childhood. You'll have to remember it all and use everything against it to destroy it. The girl will help you."

His mom swiveled around and started toward one of the doors. The one he presumed belonged to her world.

"Wait! Mom!"

She didn't stop walking until she reached the door.

"Why did you leave me?" he asked, the question that had lingered with him since she died.

"I didn't leave you, Peter," she said without turning to face him. "I'm always with you."

Unshed tears of mourning filtered out from his eyes. "I'm so sorry, Mom. I should have fought harder for you. Maybe then you wouldn't have—"

"Don't you think that for one more second," she said, looking at him over her shoulder. "You were a still a child. But, now you're grown, and you have a job to do. I've seen all the possible outcomes from your upcoming trials, and I trust you will choose your course of action wisely. Don't let yourself be deceived."

"I don't understand," he said, growing frustrated at her riddles.

"It's time for you to walk, Peter." She touched her fingers to her lips, blew him a kiss, and passed through the door in front of her without opening it.

"No! Don't leave!" He didn't bother to restrain his shouting. "I don't know what you mean!"

In response, the room spun once more. He tried to get to the door she had gone through, but he lost track of it in the movements. He wobbled toward the wall, his off-kilter equilibrium not allowing him to walk straight. His knees hit the floor first, then his hands as he fell forward. The floor bottomed out, and he spiraled into a black pit of nothingness.

Chapter Twenty

Peter jolted awake, but not in his room where he remembered falling asleep. The familiar face next to the bed only added to his confusion.

"Hannah," he said.

Her face lit up with a large smile. "You're awake!"

He glanced around the room, taking inventory of the IV stand and curtain around his bed. "Where am I?"

"The clinic. You had a seizure a few hours ago."

Peter focused his thoughts, but had no memory of the seizure.

"You don't remember?"

He shook his head. "I never do."

"What's the last thing you do remember?"

His forehead creased. A wisp of a memory floated through his mind. Staring into the gray, the thick of the evil seeping through the balcony door and pressing against his chest. Kaylen slipping her hand into his.

Then, nothing.

"I just remember looking at the gray," he said. No reason to mention Kaylen. "I woke up and looked out my bedroom window at the gray."

"She found you, you know." Hannah's cryptic tone made Peter wonder about the real reason for her statement.

"Storm must have woken her," he said. "I told her to watch that old leak around the guest room window. Must have started dripping, and she came to tell me."

She lowered her eyes. "Must have."

"I don't understand how I had a seizure to begin with. I never miss my meds."

"Doc doesn't know either. You haven't had a seizure since… I don't know how long. Junior year in high school?"

He blinked several times, stretching his memory back in time to when he last woke up in a hospital. "I think you're right." His hand patted around the sides of the bed until he found the call button and remote. He raised the head of the bed, scooting up until he was comfortable.

Hannah got up from her chair and arranged the pillow behind his head.

"No need for that," he said, despite his gratefulness. "I'm ready to go."

"Not until Doc Horton has had a good look at you." She glanced at her watch. "It's twelve past six now—"

"In the morning?"

"Yes. You've not been here very long. Once he checks you over, you can probably go home."

He threw back the covers and swung his legs over the bed. Shaking his hand with the IV needle in it, he said, "Just tell Lou Ann to get this damned thing out of me. I feel fine."

"Lou Ann isn't here today."

"Again?" Looking around the room, he noticed the absence of someone else. "Where is Kaylen?"

"Once the doc had you stabilized, she asked me to drive her back to your place. Said she had to take care of something and that you knew about it. Said you told her she could borrow your pickup."

Peter froze. What the hell was that girl up to? Stolen plates, and now she practically stole his truck. But, until he had answers, he couldn't let on that the situation had gotten that far out of control. If word got around, people might start to question his leadership and role as sheriff of Nowhere. "Yeah, I remember now."

"Why is she staying with you?"

He cleared his throat and prayed for an interruption before the topic got too far down the track. "Best way to keep her safe."

"Keep her… Peter, what are you talking about?"

Staring into Hannah's eyes, he decided honesty was best. She knew how to keep her mouth shut. "Between us?"

"Of course."

"Someone ran her off the road. That's how she had her accident. Then, two nights ago, after I took her to the inn, someone tried to break into her room."

Hannah's mouth opened, but no words came out.

"I didn't know where else to take her after that, so I let her stay at my place in the guest room. I figured it was the only way to keep an eye on her."

"I had no... Oh, my... The poor thing."

He laid his hand on hers. "Just don't tell anyone. I don't know who did these things, and I don't need the whole town knowing where she is."

The door to his room opened. Ollie walked in, with Doc Horton in tow. "I thought I heard talking in here," Ollie said, a smirk on his face. "You know, there are better ways to get a day off."

Peter chuckled despite the situation. "Yes, I realize that now."

"Feeling better?" Doc Horton asked, walking around the other side of his bed.

"Much. Ready to get out of here."

"I'll leave you all," Hannah said. "I can't leave Carlos in charge of the diner for too long. He might start thinking of taking over." She leaned over Peter, and her lips brushed his forehead. With her hand on top of his head, she said. "You get well, you hear?"

He winked and smiled. "Save some dinner for me."

She waved and exited the room.

"So, can I take him now?" Ollie asked.

"I'll give him one more glance over, make sure he's fit for duty," Doc Horton said. "But, shouldn't be an issue with him going home, so long as he takes it easy the next couple days."

"Before you do that," Ollie said, "can we have a minute? Business, you know."

The doctor moved to the door. "Just open it up when you're ready for me." He closed the door behind him.

Ollie lowered himself into the chair Hannah had occupied. "'Fraid I got some bad news for ya."

Peter's muscles instantly tensed. "What is it?"

"Tanya Whitaker's dead."

Peter jumped in the bed. "What? How? We just saw her yesterday."

"Details are a bit fuzzy still, but she went out to her mom's out in Rose Hill yesterday afternoon. Mom wasn't home, so she let herself in. Mom came home, found Tanya hanging from a rafter in the garage."

ANGIE MARTIN

"She killed herself?" As he said the words, an all-too familiar feeling passed through him. "Like Belinda killed herself."

"Yeah," Ollie said, tilting his head. "That is a bit strange now, isn't it?"

"Two suicides, a murder, and cattle mutilation all in a few days. I'd say that's more than strange."

"Something in the water?"

Peter scoffed. "Wouldn't be surprised."

"It happened out of our jurisdiction, so I didn't go to the crime scene, but the Butler County Sheriff had some questions for us about those mutilations. Wanted to know if we thought that was what drove her over the edge."

"Tanya Whitaker might have been acting strange that day, but she was not suicidal."

"That's what I told him," Ollie said. "But, I never woulda guessed that Belinda would kill Fred and herself, either."

Peter pulled in a deep breath and blew it out. His town had changed the second Kaylen had her accident, and it would never be the same again. He needed answers. His mind wandered back to the dream he had of his mom, but his recall of it didn't feel like a dream. More like a sharp memory.

It's time for you to walk, Peter.

The words stood out more than anything else his mom had said, but the mystery behind them remained.

The girl will help you.

There seemed to be only one person who could make sense of everything. And, she had just stolen his pickup truck.

Chapter Twenty-one

The two most stolen items in the history of Nowhere were dogs and pickup trucks. As sheriff, Peter knew this statistic well and had taken his own precautions. Like most Midwestern small-town men, his truck was his baby. With the advances in technology, just about any vehicle could contain GPS tracking, and he had ensured his own truck had the best there was to offer. It took one phone call and all of eleven minutes to find out where Kaylen had driven his truck.

Pulling into the driveway of the rundown bungalow in El Dorado, Peter didn't know what to expect. After parking behind his truck, he hopped out of his patrol car and raced up the front steps of the home. He didn't know if he was more angry or desperate for answers, but he decided to not bother with the doorbells and courtesies. He tried the doorknob, and it twisted. Pushing the door open, he held back the urge to announce his arrival.

Kaylen was not in the living room off to the right, but instead of searching the house further for her, he ventured into the room. Simplistic furnishings screamed that the home was not used often, except for the mass of papers scattered on the coffee table. In the middle of the mess, he spied a manila folder with his name written on the tab. He picked it up, but before opening it, he moved the rest of the pile around, uncovering photographs of him walking and driving the streets of Nowhere.

"What the hell?" he muttered to himself. He opened the folder and almost dropped it. The dossier was his life in a file. As he flipped through documents, he found his name, address, social security number, work history. At first, he thought it was identity theft, until he read through his medical records. No identity thief would need to know about his seizures as a child.

Another folder on the table caught his attention, but instead of his name, the tab read, "Arlene Holbrook." His mother. Opening the file, he read about her stay at the mental institution his father had locked her in. The one she died in when Peter was only a child.

A door on the other side of the room opened, and Kaylen walked into the living room. She stopped short when she saw Peter. "How… how did you find me?"

"GPS tracking," he said.

"I'm sorry," she said, taking a few steps forward. "When you had your seizure, I remembered this place. I should have waited for you—"

"You mean instead of stealing my truck? Like you stole the plates on that car you wrecked? I should be arresting you right now."

"I don't know what to say. It was impulsive to do that and come here, and—"

"What is this?" Peter asked, holding the file on him up for her to see.

"I don't know," she said. "I don't remember—"

"Damn it, you have to remember!"

She stepped back until the wall stopped her. "But, I don't—"

He flung the file open and held it in front of her face. "This is about me, this whole file. Were you stalking me? Targeting me for something?"

Her eyes darted back and forth from the right to left side of the file, but she didn't answer.

Peter yanked the file back and moved toward her. "What are you doing with all of my information? My medical history? My grade cards from elementary school? And, why do you have records from my mom's hospitalization?"

"I don't know, Peter. Please—"

He smacked the file against her chest, and she jumped. "This ends now," he said and walked away. He sat on the couch and thrust his hands into his hair. Anger slowly gave way to stress, which tensed every muscle in his neck and shoulders. The moment he found the files, he should have left her there, driven back to Nowhere, and forget he ever met her. But, something held him back. The same something that kept pushing them together.

"Peter, I didn't…" Kaylen inched her way across the room,

tears and caution filling her eyes. "I don't know what this is, but I know it can't be malicious."

"How do you know that?"

She paused, her mouth ajar, but no words emerged. She eased herself down into the couch cushions, leaving plenty of space between them. Lifting the file, she opened the cover and gasped at the contents. Her head rotated side to side, as if not believing what she read.

She turned a few more pages in the file. "Oh, no." Her words emerged from quivering lips, her voice deep, shaky.

"What?" he asked.

"No, no, no." The file tumbled from her fingers, the pages scattering across the carpet. "This can't be right. It can't be…"

Peter turned to face her and grabbed her arms. "What is it?"

"I remember." Her eyes inched up until they latched onto his. "God help me, I remember everything."

Chapter Twenty-two

Peter's anger over the files filtered out of his pores as quickly as it had entered his body. He let go of Kaylen's arms and sat next to her on the couch. He had been much too hard on her, but it seemed his file had stimulated her lost memories. Whatever had been locked up in her mind could provide the answers he sought.

Kaylen wrapped her arms around her trembling body. Goosebumps coated her bare arms, and her hands slid over them in an attempt to warm herself up.

Sensing her distress, Peter picked up a plush throw from the arm of the couch. He wrapped it around her shoulders, and she accepted the kind act with a smile.

"Why don't you slowly tell me what you remember?" he asked. "You don't have to rush anything, Kaylen. I want you to be comfortable."

"My name's not Kaylen," she said.

Peter jerked back. She had been so sure of her name that the revelation of a different one caught him off-guard. "What is your name?"

"Katelynn," she said. "Kaylen is what one of my friends called me when we were kids. He had a speech impediment, so all my friends just called me that from there out."

Her explanation struck him as sincere. Her mind had recalled the nickname her friends lovingly called her, something that gave her comfort and warmth while living without memory of anything else.

"Katelynn it is, then," Peter said.

"No," she said. "Call me Kaylen. Please. I haven't gone by Katelynn since… since before the…" Her voice cracked with her last words.

"Since before the what?"

"Since before I was tattooed."

He placed a tender hand on her shoulder. "Why don't we leave?" he asked. When she looked at him with surprise, he said, "We can go get something to eat, go back to my place, and take this one step at a time. We don't have to tackle all this right now."

"No, I want to do this. I need to do this now. Sort through the memories and get it all out."

The resolve and strength in her voice convinced Peter. "That's fine, too. Whatever you want."

"Water."

Peter cocked his head to the side. "Excuse me?"

"I think I need some water."

She started to stand, but he stopped her. "You just rest. I'll get you some."

Her warm smile thanked him, and he made his way to the kitchen. He checked the cupboard closest to the empty stainless-steel sink first and found glasses. He pulled out two of the tall ones and set them down on the spotless granite countertop. Opening the freezer, he paused. Only two ice cube trays peeked back at him. He grabbed one of them and set it next to the glasses. Out of curiosity, he opened the refrigerator. A six-pack of beer bottles, two of which were missing, sat haphazardly angled in the middle of the top shelf. Nothing else.

Peter shook his head as he shut the door. The mystery of Kaylen ran deeper than a missing – now recovered – memory.

Armed with ice water, he returned to the living room. He sat on the couch next to her as she devoured the entire glass of water as if she had been without it for days. She set the glass down on the coffee table and sighed.

"I don't know where to begin," she said. She swung her gaze to his face. "I've wasted so much time not remembering."

"Just start where you think it's best."

"You're in danger, Peter."

He slowly leaned back against the couch, staring at her intent eyes, taking in her words.

"I'm sorry to say it like that, but there's no other way. I don't know how much time we have left until…" Her hand flew to her mouth. "If everything is too far along, we may not be able to stop it at all. Oh, no… Shane!"

"Okay," Peter said. "Slow down. Who is Shane?"

"I need to use your phone. I know I have one, but I don't know where—"

"Here," he said, pulling his cell phone out of his pocket and handing it to her.

She grabbed it and punched in a number, one Peter knew he'd have to trace later. "Shane, it's me." She stopped speaking, and Peter heard a male voice coming through the other end. Yelling, from the sound of it. "I know, I know! Just give me a damn minute to explain. Someone ran me off the road when I got to town." She paused for a long moment. "Yeah, yeah, I figured that's what happened." Another pause. "I must have hit my head pretty hard 'cause I lost my memory, but it's back now."

Peter strained his ears, but couldn't make out what the man was saying.

"No, I'm with the sheriff now." She raised her eyes to look at Peter. "Yeah, I'll tell him everything. We don't have any time to waste. I'll keep you posted." She disconnected the call and handed the phone back to Peter. "I'm sorry about that. I knew he'd be worried—"

"Who is Shane?"

"I'll explain everything back at your house," she said. "Right now, we need to grab as much info as we can and get out of here. Whoever knows I'm in town may have followed me here."

Though curiosity crushed through him, he followed her lead. "What do you need?"

"Get all those files from the table. I have to find my laptop." She wandered back in the bedroom, while he worked on gathering the files and paperwork from the table.

"Found my phone," she said, holding it up. She carried a laptop case in her other hand. Glancing at the coffee table, she asked, "You get them all?"

"Yeah," he said.

"I'll take the truck, and you can follow me back to your house. We might have to take the long way to make sure no one is following us. Who knows I'm staying with you?"

"Uh…" Her authoritative tone caught him off-guard. "Hannah knows, but that's it."

"Good. We won't come back here in case someone followed

me."

"Won't you need to—"

"It's just a rental, and we have all the important things. How could I have been so careless?"

"You kinda lost your memory there," he said. "Don't be so hard on yourself. I just wish I knew what was going on."

"I'm sorry. I know it's like a tornado going through your life right now, and I wish I could change that. But, I promise, I'll tell you everything at your house."

He nodded, realizing he had little choice but to accept it. He followed her out the front door, bracing himself for whatever was to come.

Chapter Twenty-three

Kaylen steered them through backroads Peter thought only locals knew about. Armed with her warning of possible followers, he kept his eye on the rearview mirror, but didn't see anyone stay behind them for long enough to consider them a threat of any kind.

Back at his house, they carried in Kaylen's belongings and set up in his living room. While she sorted through some of the paperwork from her house, he settled into the recliner next to the couch and read through his mom's file, reliving the worst months of his childhood.

"I dreamt about my mom last night," he said off-the-cuff. He wasn't even sure if he said it loud enough for Kaylen to hear until he heard her answer.

"Before or after your seizure?" she asked.

"After. I woke up from the dream in the hospital." He lifted the file and said, "You seem to know all about her."

"Then why don't you tell me about her? Let me hear it from you."

"She's important to this, isn't she?" He didn't wait for a reply. "I was just starting my freshman year in high school when she was sent away. Dad thought she was talking crazy all the time, and one day she was gone. He said she went to the hospital to get better, but the one time he let me see her, I knew it was a mental institution."

"How was she talking crazy?"

"Talking about demons. Saying they lived in the gray. That one day they would come to Nowhere, and that I'd have to walk. She was obsessed with me walking. The last days she was at home, she'd tell me constantly. She said that in my dream, too. That it was time for me to walk. I don't have any idea what she meant by that."

If the revelations startled Kaylen, she didn't show it in her face. "How long was she institutionalized before she died?"

"Four months. I still don't know how she died for sure. They say it was her heart, but that never made sense to me."

"Didn't make sense to me, either," Kaylen said. "Unfortunately, I can't find anything to prove otherwise."

Just the idea that she had been investigating his mom's death unnerved him. "Tell me what's going on. Please."

"Your mom wasn't crazy, Peter. Demons do live in the gray, but they can't manifest themselves without a human host, a vessel strong enough to contain them. That lady we saw yesterday. What was her name?"

"Tanya Whitaker."

"She wasn't just acting odd. She was possessed by a demon. That's the behavior I recognized. I've seen it a hundred times before."

"She hung herself last night."

"Not surprising. Your friend who died? I bet she was also possessed when she killed her husband and herself."

Peter shook his head. Kaylen said everything matter-of-factly, as if he should just accept her word. Even though it seemed to make sense – with all the odd behavior and the deaths – the last time someone he knew spoke about demons, it resulted in her being locked away.

"Let me see if I have this right," he said. "People in my town are being possessed by demons and going crazy?"

"Human souls are not built to contain that kind of evil. Yes, we are all capable of sin, and great sin at that, but a demon is a different kind of evil than what humans can even dream of. Demons are fallen angels, after all."

"They fell with Lucifer after rebelling against God. One-third of angels, if I remember right."

"Angels are already powerful beings, ones humans can barely look at. The Bible is littered with stories of how those interactions go. Now, imagine an evil angel – a demon – possessing a body. If the demon can hold on tight enough, it can remain in someone indefinitely. Most people can't handle it, though, so it's finding people who can handle that possession in the first place that's so difficult."

"So, if a person can't handle the demon possession, they start acting differently?"

"Exactly. What else has happened in town recently? Either before or after your friends' deaths."

"Well, the cattle mutilations yesterday."

"Classic demon infestation sign. Carnage of any kind, really, but livestock usually end up on the receiving end."

"A few others have been acting weird in town. Lou Ann from the clinic. Another guy, Lyle Shepard. Maybe some others I don't know about."

"Lou Ann? Probably a demon trying to stop me because I'd stayed there. Anything else?"

"Belinda's baby was stillborn. That's what we thought caused her to kill Fred and herself."

"That makes sense. If she was already possessed when she gave birth, there's no way an innocent child could survive that." She let out a low whistle. "This is so far along now."

"How do you know all this? I mean, I'm having a hard time even believing these things happened, and you just act like it's just another Thursday."

"I know, and I wish I had time to let this simmer with you. Normally, I don't go around talking about demons and such without being able to ease someone into it all."

"So, what? You hunt down demons?"

"Yeah, I do."

"And, that Shane guy you called?"

"He's like my boss. He finds demon cases and sends people like me out on jobs."

"Is that what the tattoos are about? Some kind of demon hunter's club?"

"No." She held out her arms, looking them over. "Those are a story for another day."

"I'd prefer to know it today." At her hesitance, Peter continued. "You just gave me a lot of crazy information about demons and told me they're invading my town. Strangely, it makes a lot of sense to me, what, with everything that's happened around here and the things my mom talked about when I was a kid, but you gotta give me more to go on here."

"I need a drink," she said, standing up. "Do you have any beer?"

"Uh…" He had to think for a moment not expecting her question. "Yeah, there's a couple in the fridge. Help yourself."

She disappeared into the kitchen, returning moments later with two open Budweiser bottles. Handing one to Peter, she said, "I figured you need one as much as I do."

His eyebrows arched as he accepted the beer. The bitter, somewhat bland chilled liquid slid down his throat like a refreshing glass of water. When he finally lowered the bottle, it was half-drained.

Kaylen laughed. "Yup, you needed that."

"I suppose I did." He twisted the bottle in his hand. "I don't really talk about my mom."

"I don't really talk about my tattoos."

He caught her eyes and could see her unease. "It's that bad?"

"Worse." She set her beer down on the coffee table next to her laptop. Leaning back, she sighed. "My parents started practicing Wicca before I was born. After a while, the coven they belonged to desired more power. One of the witches started reading *The Satanic Bible*, and they all got involved in it. They started combining the two: witchcraft and Satanism. Then, they incorporated parts of Aleister Crowley's teachings of Thelema. They were ever-evolving. Rituals and spells… anything they could feed off. Whatever made them more powerful as a coven."

Peter frowned. "Witchcraft doesn't actually work, though, does it? Spells and magic… I mean, that stuff isn't real, is it?"

"It is, and they do work, but not because of what people think. It's all tied to demonology. Demons control black magic. By granting spells and fueling witches, they all but guarantee the soul of the witch belongs to them for all of eternity."

"And, your parents were part of this coven?"

"They weren't just part of it; they started the coven and were the driving force behind everything it did. I was raised in the coven by all the witches. I floated from house to house and was able to perform spells from the time I was three."

"That's so young."

"My parents say it's because of the way I was conceived, during a black magic ritual. They intended for me to be the heir to the coven and the most powerful witch in history."

Her words chilled him, but he pressed her for more. "Is that why you're tattooed?"

"Not exactly. See, when you invite demons to play in your life, they will take over everything. They'll entwine themselves so much in your everyday that ridding yourself of them is almost impossible. It was no surprise to anyone that on the eve of my twelfth birthday, a demon took full control over me."

"You were possessed?"

She nodded. "The coven pushed for the demon to possess me. It had been working on me for quite some time, but I refused to let it in. I knew what my parents – what the coven – did was wrong, but I had to pretend to follow along. When you're a kid, you don't exactly want to be kicked out of the house with no place to go. I fought the demon with everything I had, but it wasn't enough. Even a child as powerful as I was couldn't resist a demon forever.

"The coven was thrilled at first, but it didn't take long for them to regret it. The demon controlled everything I did. I was just a passenger, watching from the inside. Eventually, it killed two dissenting members of the coven."

His mouth fell open, but no words emerged. Most of what she said was foreign to him, but having to watch herself kill two people without any control… He couldn't fathom how awful it must have been for her.

"It was then that they realized they had to stop the demon. They tried everything. Six different exorcisms were performed. Excruciating exorcisms. Then, someone came up with the idea for the tattoos."

"So, what? The tattoos keep the demon from returning?"

"No, Peter. The exorcisms, and everything else they tried, failed. The demon had latched onto my soul in a way that they couldn't force it out. They had two options. One was to kill me to dispel the demon, but the demon would never let that happen. The other was to trap the demon and limit its power so I could take back control."

His gaze latched onto her single dark eye, the same color that had flashed in Keith's eyes when he had gone crazy in the jail cell. Peter finally understood. "The demon is still in you? It still possesses you?"

"It's inside of me, but because of the tattoos, I can control it, for the most part."

"Is that why your eyes are different colors?"

She pointed to her dark eye. "This eye was blue before it possessed me, then they both turned to black while I was possessed.

After the tattoos, the other one returned to blue, but not this one. This is the eye the demon sees the world through."

He shuddered and reached for his beer. "It can see everything? It's seeing me right now?"

"Yes. Those headaches I was having when the memories were coming back. They weren't really headaches, but I was too afraid to say anything. It was the demon's voice talking to me, telling me things." She gestured to her head. "It was painful, hearing it, and I didn't know what it was at the time. I thought I was losing my mind."

Without thought, he jumped out of the recliner and sat next to her on the couch. Laying his hand on her arm, he said, "I wish you would have told me. I know it would have been risky, but I've seen and heard enough strange things in my life that I might just have believed you."

A long moment passed before she murmured, "Thank you. You don't know how much that means to me. I have to convince so many people I'm not crazy that… Just, thank you."

Before removing his hand from her arm, he looked down at the tattoos and ran his fingertips over them. "You said these tattoos were done when you were a kid? They all look so fresh."

"The ink was spelled – a powerful, binding spell. It made it so the tattoos would never fade. Also, no one can replicate them. That's why your phone couldn't take a picture of them. It's all part of the spell. They didn't want to take any chances that the demon could hurt someone else."

"Is there any chance the demon can be exorcised?"

"With the tattoos, probably not. But, there is an ancient spell book, the grimoire of a powerful witch from the 1300's. Grimoires didn't become common until the eighteenth century, so this one is said to be the oldest of its kind. It may contain the spells I need to rid myself of the tattoos and the demon."

"You haven't tried yet?"

"We can't find it. Shane is always searching, but I've mostly given up hope."

"Don't give up hope," he said, giving her arm a squeeze before letting go.

She looked down with a slight nod. "We have a lot of work to do, Peter, if we're going to save this town and get you in the clear."

"Where do we start?"

"I suggest we finish off these beers and grab something to eat before it gets too late. As soon as the sun goes down, it'll be time for you to walk." She rose from the couch and, with the beer bottle sealed to her lips, she walked into the kitchen, ending the conversation for the moment.

Chapter Twenty-four

W ho would have thought a small Kansas town would have Chinese food this good?"

Peter laughed as he twirled his fork through the Lo Mein on his plate. He had ordered and picked it up from a town forty-five minutes away, limiting the chances they would run into anyone who may be searching for Kaylen. "There's probably a lot you don't know about small towns in Kansas. Where are you from anyway?"

"Lots of places," she said. "Raised in Arizona, but I don't really claim it as home. Not since I have no one to visit."

"Do you know where your parents are now?"

"No, and I don't care to know. What they did was inexcusable, no matter how sorry they are." She took a swig of her beer. "Are you a lifer here in Kansas?"

"Oh, yeah. Can't imagine myself anywhere else in the world. This is my town, demons and all." He pushed his plate aside on the kitchen table. "Is it ever going to be back to normal here, or are demons now the norm?"

Kaylen stared at him for a moment, as if formulating an answer. Instead of responding, she picked up a fortune cookie and tossed it at him.

He ripped open the cellophane wrapper. "Don't you hate it when you get a fortune cookie that's not a fortune?"

"Like the ones that are sayings or telling you something you already know?" She laughed and grabbed one for herself. "One of my biggest pet peeves."

Cracking open his cookie, he unfolded the paper. The smile on his face dropped as he read the non-fortune.

"I take it you didn't get a fortune," Kaylen said, cracking open her own cookie.

"'Walking good form exercise.'" He glanced up at her, and noticed her expression had also sobered upon reading hers. "What does yours say?"

"'No time like present.'"

"Huh." Peter set the cookie down on his plate. "Does God speak to people through fortune cookies now?"

"Looks like it." Without discussion, they both rose from the kitchen table, leaving dirty dishes and leftovers for cleanup later, and moved to the living room. Once seated on the couch, Kaylen asked, "Do you believe in God?"

Though the question came out of nowhere, Peter didn't hesitate to answer. "Of course."

"There's a difference between believing in God and knowing there is a God. For a long time, I knew there was a God. I had a demon living inside me, so there *had* to be a God. It took me some time to actually believe."

"I believe," Peter said firmly.

"Good. You need to."

"You sound like you've doubted Him before, which I can understand, given your childhood."

"It wasn't doubt so much as I used to get upset with Him, wondering why He didn't take this fight with demons more seriously. Why didn't He get His hands dirty on the battleground more often? But, I've learned that it isn't my place to question. He was always there more than my human mind could even begin to comprehend, even during my childhood. He's been here during this demon activity as well. The seizure you had, followed by the dream of your mom. The seizure jogged my memory enough for it to return. Your mom's visit, whether it was real or just a dream, prepared you for everything to come. Those things… well, there's no other way to explain them other than divine intervention."

Peter thought it over. "You know, I never miss taking my epilepsy meds. Haven't had a seizure since I was in high school."

She held out her hands. "Divine intervention. The seizure happened despite you being on your meds. Was your mom heavily involved with your epilepsy when you were a child?"

Peter's mother cared more about his epilepsy than even he did. It was always the same for him: take this pill, no, try this one, or maybe this one. The pill-switching ritual, with all its terrible side effects, went on for years, until the newest medication worked. They waited and when no seizures came, the doctor declared Peter stable. Peter took his two pills every day, went to regular checkups for his refills, and that was that. No reason to ever dwell on the illness.

"She always was involved," Peter said. "She stayed on top of everything, questioned the doctors. Whatever needed to be done to stabilize me."

"There was one seizure in your medical history that caught my attention. You spent some time in the hospital."

"Yes, when I was in junior high." He knew immediately to which time she referred. It was *that* seizure. The one that seemed to hang over him, even as an adult. One moment, he was racing across the park chasing Hannah after school. She wore her copper hair in a ponytail that day. It bounced off the back of her yellow polo shirt with fluffy sleeve caps. Her slender legs, encased in dark blue jeans, ran as fast as they could while he followed in their daily game of tag, under the monkey bars, dodging other kids swinging, and finally through the soccer field while avoiding getting run over themselves. He laughed, she laughed. The spring air burst with the sound of their young love in full bloom.

The next thing he knew, he had awakened in a hospital bed. His mom's creased face appeared over his, then several other concerned adults followed. Not his dad – *never* his dad – but others came in and out of the room. It was as if he had come back from the dead.

"Do you remember anything from that day?" Kaylen asked, as if having witnessed his memories first-hand.

"They said I died," he said without the slightest inflection in his tone. "I don't think they wanted me to know, but I overheard the doctor talking to my mom in the hallway."

The warmth of her hand settled on his, luring his eyes up to her face, which mirrored the concerned faces of all those adults in his hospital room that day. "You did die, Peter," she said. "You crossed over, and you came back."

Her words shook him, more than anything had ever rumbled his body. He *had* died that day. He had crossed the bridge into the hereafter, possibly saw the face of God, and he remembered nothing.

Peter strained his mind, stretched his memory to its snapping point, but nothing came. No memory of a white light, no overwhelming feeling of love. Nothing but a hole in his life. The park, a hole, the hospital. If he could remember just a little, maybe get a glimpse of Heaven, if he could see where his mother now resided, he would know she was okay.

"You will never remember," Kaylen said, once again reading his mind. "If you don't already know what happened, it won't come back. But, something in you changed that day."

"I crossed over," he said, his mind stuck in a loop of trying to retrieve his memory.

"More than that, Peter."

"The gray," he whispered. He rose from the couch and glided to the front window on feet that did not seem to belong to him. Pulling back the curtain and peering into the nothingness of the rain, he said, "I could feel the gray. I could feel *them* in the gray."

"We need to find out who else can feel them."

"It must be someone who also crossed over," Peter said without turning around.

"Or, someone who summoned them. I think it's time we try walking."

His attention snagged, he turned around and moved back to the couch. Resting his hands on the back of it, he said, "The mysterious walking."

"It's not what you think. Walking is allowing your soul to leave your body."

"Like an out-of-body experience?"

"Exactly that."

"What makes you think I can do that, and why would I want to?"

"You crossed over, Peter. You've already walked between the doors of life and death. Your soul already knows how to leave your body. It just needs some coaxing."

"The last time my soul left my body, I died."

"You won't die, I promise. You're just going to let your soul walk and then return to your body. We should at least experiment and make sure it's possible."

"I still haven't heard the 'why' to this experiment."

"I think you can see the demons when you walk. We can't see them while we're in human form, but your soul can see them. It can *sense* them, leading us right to them. Any other way of tracking them is too dangerous, takes too long, and is not guaranteed to work."

"But, wouldn't they see me?"

She shook her head. "I don't think so. You'll be mostly invisible to them. They only see other demons and the living when they are in human form. As long as you stay at a distance, they shouldn't recognize your spirit and you'll be safe."

"That doesn't sound too safe to me."

"That's the beauty of walking. Your soul can see further and hear more than your restricted human body, so you can stay a good distance away while identifying who they've possessed."

His heart raced out of control while his mind spun a million reasons why he shouldn't try walking. "I don't know, Kaylen. How would I find my way back?"

"You should be able to find your way back since you'll still be alive, but just in case, I'll do a spell to tether you to your body."

"Magic? Spells? Hell, I didn't know those things were real until today."

"You question spells after all you've been through these past few days? After everything you've seen?"

He chuckled, letting some of the stress flow from his body. "Spells are where I draw the line." He took a deep breath. "Okay, so you do a spell to keep me attached to my body. That all sounds great, but what about the demons themselves?"

"I think for this first time, we just practice walking. Demons are nothing to scoff at. When you walk tonight, you'll be able to see my demon and at least get used to what they look like. That way it won't take you by surprise when you find the others."

Knowing Kaylen had a demon inside of her and seeing it were worlds apart as far as Peter was concerned. He still had a hard time grasping the concept that she was possessed. "Are you sure that's safe?"

"Absolutely. My demon is stuck inside of me. It will be able to see you because you'll be so close to me, but it can't hurt you. It might... well, it *will* speak to you. Try to trick you or tell you things, but as long as you are aware of that and you don't respond, you'll be fine."

"Great. So, prepare me a little here. What do they look like?"

"I wish I could tell you, but they look different to different people. They take on the forms that will most startle someone. My demons have holes where their eyes should be and no mouths or noses."

"That dream you had," Peter said. "You were seeing memories of demons."

"Yes, but what you see will look completely different. I've seen enough to know how terrifying they can be, even if you're used to them. Just remember that my demon can't hurt you. It is very well contained and has no power."

"Do you walk to see demons?"

"I don't have that ability like you do. But, during an exorcism, it's a natural reaction for the demon's true form to come through and overshadow the possessed. They can also show themselves if they want."

Peter's mind raced with more questions, but he swallowed back his fear. No amount of talking would make it any easier, nor would it change the situation. "Let's do this, before I change my mind."

Chapter Twenty-five

Following Kaylen's instructions to get comfortable, Peter settled down on the couch, lying on his back. They had moved the coffee table out of the way, and Kaylen sat in a kitchen chair she moved in front of the couch. From the corner of his eye, he watched her knees jitter up and down.

"You're making me nervous," he said.

Her movement halted. "Sorry," she said. "I'm nervous myself. I've never done this before."

"I don't know how I can leave my body. The concept of it alone…" He shook his head. "It sounds crazy."

"My theory is that since you've done it before, it will come naturally. We just have to get you in the right state to do it. Close your eyes."

He complied and shook his body to try and relax. A soft touch on his cheek startled his eyes open. Kaylen leaned over him, the heat from her hands on either side of his face boring into his skin.

"I'm sorry," she said. "I forgot to warn you that when I spell you, I need to touch you. I hope that's okay."

His heart hitched on something… some emotion he wasn't familiar with attributing to anyone else than Hannah. It resumed beating after a moment, but with an arrhythmia he couldn't control. Something in her porcelain skin, her single blue eye – something about the shape of her lips – it all caused electricity to surge through his veins. He half-expected her to lower her face to his, and he *wanted* her to, wanted to experience her kiss and discover where it would take them.

Instead, she withdrew her hands and moved back in her chair.

"Do you have one of those touch phobias?"

Crap. She had taken his silence to mean he didn't enjoy her touch, when he enjoyed it a little too much. "No," he said. "I was caught a little off-guard, but it's fine. Do what you need to." He cringed at his sterile words. No wonder he remained the eternal bachelor.

She nodded and scooted to the edge of the chair again. Her hands hovered next his face, on either side. "Ready?"

"Let's do this." He closed his eyes again, but this time, a bit more tense knowing her fingers would soon caress his skin.

When she did touch him, he instinctively shifted his face into her palm, but she didn't stop. Her thumbs covered his eyelids and moved in sporadic directions. He tried to understand what they were doing, but couldn't make out anything. He assumed it to be some sort of symbol that matched the low-toned foreign language she spoke. Part of the spell.

Despite his overactive mind attempting to decipher her movements over his eyelids and interpret what language she spoke – Latin, perhaps? – his body seemed to sink into the couch. His muscles had never been more relaxed.

After a few minutes, Peter gave up on the spell working. He opened his eyes and sat up. Strangely, Kaylen didn't move back to give him room. His lips parted to speak, but he stopped. His neck twisted to the left, and he jumped back at the sight of his body on the couch. She still leaned over him, still held her hands on his face, but he could no longer feel it.

Standing up, he realized his legs weren't solid, nor did they look normal. The edges were fuzzy, giving it an odd shape, though the center mass still held the general appearance of a leg. *This is my spirit,* he thought. *This is how God sees me.*

The idea exploded in his brain, and he started to panic. Though the attack began in his mind, he quickly noticed his chest didn't heave up and down with shallow breaths. He didn't breathe at all. He put his hand over his heart, but no beat came with it. Was he dead? Had he died during the spell?

Looking back at Kaylen, she eased away from him and settled into her chair. She folded her arms across her lap and watched Peter's body. If he had died, she would have been on the phone with emergency services.

Spirits don't need to breathe. Of course… why would they?

Nothing about his spirit form would be the same as his human form. The thought helped him settle into his current state, and he moved to where Kaylen sat. Bending over before her, he inspected her face. He had expected to immediately see the demon inside her, but she appeared normal.

He lifted his cupped hand and pressed it to her face. She gasped when he connected with her, but she didn't move beyond that, as if she sensed his touch but couldn't fully feel it. He pushed into her skin, but it didn't dimple like it should have with a solid hand. Her face felt more spongey than anything, but he couldn't completely determine the texture.

Wondering what else might be different, he decided to explore the living room. At first, it all seemed the same. Furniture in the right places, his mom's framed photo on the fireplace mantel, clock and pictures on the wall. But, something in the corner of the room caught his attention, and he walked over to investigate. A glint of light, not much larger than a pinpoint, hung in the air. It rolled back and forth, side to side, and diagonal, then moving in all different directions at random.

He swiped his fingers through the light, and it brightened and grew. His eyes widened as he stepped backward. The light shifted and changed until it spanned from floor to ceiling in a rectangular shape. A golden knob, brighter than any painted metal at the hardware store, appeared on the right side, where one would belong on a door. He reached for the knob without hesitation, but it wouldn't twist beyond an inch, as if the door was locked. The resistance frustrated him, and he tried again, pushing and pulling on the door.

"Don't open the door, Peter."

Kaylen's hollow voice stopped him from twisting the knob. He whirled around, expecting to see her staring at him, but her gaze remained on his still form resting on the couch.

Something flicked across her eyes. A shadow, a cloud... he couldn't be certain. He moved to her and sat on the edge of the couch, careful not to sit on his body. He focused on her eyes, on the strange black fog that floated in front of them. It swirled for a moment, a black hole sucking in everything that dared to look too closely, and then it stopped and hovered in front of her eyes, as if it suddenly became aware of him.

A second skin appeared over hers, like a drop shadow that

perfectly mimicked her face. Where her human form remained in one place, the secondary face, an exact replica of her own features, shifted and changed independent of her solid form. He realized it must be her spirit, caught within her body.

The second-hand on the wall clock ticked, the sound so loud it shook the room around him. He jumped off the couch and walked to the clock. The wood stretched as it grew, distorting its proportions until it fell from the wall. The clock face stared up at him, the now-jagged second-hand ticking, ticking, ticking… until it stopped and moved backward, just by one second.

The silence that overcame the room threatened to deafen him, until he heard Kaylen's voice again. "Open the door, Peter." This time, her tone had no inflection, and, for a moment, he doubted she spoke. But, the lips of her spirit moved in his direction. "It's okay, Peter. Just open the door."

The door flashed in his periphery, but he ignored it. Back at the couch and sat in front of her, staring down the demon that looked identical to Kaylen. "You're not her," he said.

What he initially thought was her spirit smiled at him. He could smell the sinister intentions forming on her tongue, the decay and rot that he imagined only a demon could produce.

"Time is a curious thing," it said. "In here, in The Between, it means absolutely nothing. It could go forward. It could go backward. It could go diagonal. It wouldn't matter to anyone how time ticks in here. As long as it tick, tick, ticks." It clicked its tongue at the end of each "tick."

Peter wanted to speak, he had so many questions, but he remembered Kaylen's admonition not to respond to it.

"Do you believe in gravity, Peter?"

Peter squinted his eyes with curiosity. In a blink, the room turned upside-down. Furniture floated through the air, and his own body was dislodged from the couch, spinning somewhere over the airborne television set. Vertigo racked his soul, and he reached out to try to grab hold of something. In his panic, he couldn't find anything to steady himself.

He blinked again, and the room returned to normal. He wobbled on the couch where he was seated, but quickly regained control.

"Nothing in The Between is what it seems. I can control it, you know. It bends and twists with my every whim. I don't have to move at all; I simply have to think it, and it happens. I am a god in here. I might even be your god, if you stay here long enough with me. And, I so want you to stay here with me."

Peter shifted his gaze back to the demon, his eyes now narrowed. "You don't scare me," he said. "I know what you're trying to do, and it won't work."

"You're right," it said. "How lazy of me to even attempt to trick you. You've seen all this before, haven't you? That day you died. The day we almost pulled you through that door."

"There is nothing you can say that will make me walk away from what I need to do." His words were far braver than his soul, but he knew he could not cave, could not bend, even a little.

"Of course," it said. "But, don't wander too far from your body. You might just join your mother with us, beyond the door."

The mention of his mom stopped Peter's thoughts for a moment, but he quickly recovered. "You're lying."

"One day, Kaylen will join us down there, too. Deep, deep down in The Below."

"No, she—"

The demon screamed, a high-pitched, multi-tonal scream that pierced through Peter's soul. Peter's hands flew to his ears, but it did nothing to deafen the sound that seemed to crackle through his spirit. Random muscles spasmed in his back, legs, arms, and chest, contorting his form and launching him forward until he fell off the couch. He writhed on the ground, the scream threatening to rupture his eardrums and explode his brain. He tried to cry out for mercy, but his vocal chords were frozen by the horrific sound.

When the noise finally ceased, Peter opened his eyes and slowly worked his way back to the couch. Once seated, he looked up to find the demon mutating before him, just under Kaylen's face. Its mouth widened until rows of jagged teeth jutted out from between its lips. Its eyes diminished into black slits that stared at Peter as if it were about to devour him. The rest of its features shifted, never quite taking form, causing vertigo to wash over Peter.

"She thinks she has me trapped," it said, its voice layered as if multiple people spoke through it, from high-pitched to low baritone. "But, I'm the one who has ensnared her. Do you know what I'm doing to her soul every day I'm inside of her? It's beautiful in here, Peter. A fantasyland of my own making. You should see it."

Anger gushed through Peter. "You're lying again."

"When she dies, I'll rip her spirit from her body and drag it down to The Below with me, where I'll feast on her for all eternity. Maybe I'll play with her a bit in The Between first. Hide the door from her sight until I grow bored."

"You don't get to decide that. You have no say where her soul goes after death."

"And, what do you care about her insignificant soul?" It laughed at him, but quickly ceased. Its face transformed again, returning to normal features, to a mirror image of Kaylen's face. "Have you developed feelings for me?"

The question, posed to him in Kaylen's voice, caught Peter off-guard. "You're not her."

"Because I think about you, Peter. I think about you a lot. During the day, in the middle of the night. Ever since I started studying your life, learning about you. Sometimes, I even dream about you."

"Stop it." But, even as he issued the command, he was curious about the demon's words. Was it being honest or dragging Peter down a dark path of lies?

"I think about you, just as much as you think about me. And, you *do* think about me, don't you, Peter? Think about all those things you want to do to this body. The things you don't talk about in the light of day because you know how disturbing it all is."

Peter forced himself to remain silent. He couldn't let the demon continue to engage him in conversation, to taunt him and wrap him up in things that would detract from saving his town. That was the demon's reason for leading him astray. Peter was sure of it.

As he tuned out the demon's droning, he wondered how to return to his body. Kaylen had failed to provide him with instructions on that part of walking. Was it supposed to come natural? Was he supposed to will himself back? He rose from the couch and turned around to face his body.

"And, where do you think you're going, boy?" The demon hissed the question.

Peter didn't respond. He closed his eyes and thought about returning to his human form, but nothing happened.

"Oooh!" The demon squealed, its eyes glowing orange-red. "You're stuck! You're stuck with me and my imagination in The Between. How marvelous! What fun we'll have together. What shall we do first? Hmm? What games shall we play?"

"Stop it." Peter spoke just above a whisper.

"I think we shall open that door first," it continued, as if Peter hadn't spoken. "Oh, Peter. Behind that door are sights that one such as yourself never get to behold!"

"Stop it." His tone was firmer, louder this time.

"We can invite some of my friends to play along. They'd love to meet you. He Who Walks Between Doors. Little Petey Holbrook. Or, do you prefer Sheriff now that you're all grown up?"

"Stop!"

As soon as the word left his lips, something tugged – *sucked* – his abdomen backward so hard, he thought his torso would be ripped in pieces if he resisted.

His eyes snapped open, and he pulled in a deep, raspy breath as if he'd been underwater too long. Kaylen sprung up from her chair and hovered over him. Her hands dove between his arms and body, and she lifted him to a sitting position.

"It's okay, Peter. You're going to be fine." Her frantic tone undermining words that were meant to comfort.

He gulped in air as if it were running out, but his lungs seemed unable to fill. He grasped Kaylen's arm for support.

"Just breathe normally," she said. "In through your nose, out through your mouth. Try to control it."

He followed her example of how to breathe, and within a few minutes, oxygen doused the fire in his lungs. His heartrate slowed to a normal rhythm, and his head stopped spinning. He leaned his head back against the couch and closed his eyes.

"Are you okay?"

"No," he said. "I'm a long way from okay."

"Did it talk to you?"

He massaged his temples, but didn't answer. He remembered the demon talking, but he was still sorting through everything it had said. Everything he had seen. "The Between," he whispered.

"That's what it's called," she said. "The space between life and death. What else did it say?"

"It called me 'He Who Walks Between Doors.'"

"It's because you died and crossed over. You walked between the doors of life and death."

"I don't know about this, Kaylen." He pushed himself up from the couch. "It's too much. With everything that's happened… I just can't take much more."

"I know it takes time to process and understand, but we're quickly running out of that luxury."

He walked over to the coatrack and grabbed his brown leather jacket. "I need to get out of here."

"You can't. We don't know yet—"

He held up his hand. "I don't care. I need to just drive and let this process. You'll be okay for a bit?"

She closed her mouth and nodded.

He picked up his keys from the table in the foyer and jangled them in his hand until he found his truck key. "I won't be long."

"Be careful, Peter."

Taking one last look at her, he thought he might catch another glimpse of her demon. When it didn't appear, he forced an awkward smile and left the house with no particular destination in mind.

Chapter Twenty-six

P eter pushed open the heavy wooden door to *The Hole*. He had spent many nights in the past enjoying a beer and dancing with other country music fanatics from town. The Hole had served Nowhere as its only bar for as long as Peter could remember. On his twenty-first birthday, his friends held a huge surprise birthday party for him there, where he consumed one too many shots of whiskey and partook in one too many line dances.

Peter smiled at the memory as he settled onto an empty barstool.

"What can I get ya, Sheriff?" Wade Young asked, flicking his overgrown brown bangs off his forehead with a sharp fling of his head.

The 22-year-old high school dropout had worked at his mom's bar since the day he turned 18. Wade's overbearing parent, Rita, was well-known to Peter, as she called the Sheriff's station on a regular basis to report even the slightest out-of-control patron. She liked to press charges at the drop of a hat, and singlehandedly kept their only courtroom busy. Wade, however, outshone his mom with his intelligence and respectful demeanor. Peter had often considered asking Wade if he had interest in getting his GED and becoming a deputy, but the young adult's immaturity held him back.

Peter scowled. "I've told you a hundred times. When I'm off duty, you can call me Peter."

Wade leaned over the bar and whispered in a confiding tone. "I know that, Sheriff, but Mama says you earned your position, and I gotta call you 'Sheriff,' even when you're off duty." He glanced over his shoulder, most likely to ensure his mother wasn't eavesdropping.

"You have a good mom there," Peter said, trying not to choke on his words. "I'll take whatever you have on tap."

"Coming right up, Sheriff."

Peter shifted his eyes to the scratches in the aging wood counter. A bit of graffiti trailed into his immediate seating area, and Peter shook his head at the stupidity. He noticed a new addition from a local drunk, Bill Collins, who had carved his name into the counter just above an obscenity. Peter shifted his elbows to cover the writing, just in case Rita wandered by and insisted on filing an immediate police report and arrest on Peter's night off.

Wade returned with a full beer glass and insisted the drink was on the house. Peter threw down a five-dollar bill anyway, and ignored Wade's objections to the tip.

Peter swiveled on his stool to take in the scene behind him. His eyes immediately focused on Hannah sitting alone at a high-top table. Her wandering gaze locked on his. Her smile gleamed at him from across the room for a long moment before she waved a hello.

Leaving his beer on the bar, Peter pushed off the stool and found his way to her table.

"How are you doing tonight, Sheriff?" she asked, the smile still glued to her lips.

"Oh, no," Peter said. "Not you, too, with this 'sheriff' nonsense."

Hannah giggled, an innocent sound that calmed his nerves. "I know how much you hate that."

Peter laughed. He started to take a seat to join her, but noticed a glass of beer opposite Hannah's mixed drink on the table. From past outings with her, he knew several of her friends drank beer. "I see you needed a night out as much as I did," he said, his gaze flicking toward the dance floor to see which friend she was out with tonight.

"It's been a rough week. How's Kaylen?" Hannah's voice brought his attention back to her.

"She's doing better. She's starting to get her memory back."

"That's great," she said, true happiness lighting her face. "Is she still staying with you?"

The question was a probe, Peter realized. "There's reason to believe she's still in danger," he said.

"You're a good man to take her in, Sheriff Holbrook."

Peter started to respond, but a voice interrupted him.

"Sorry about that," the man said from behind him. "She's in

126

bed now."

Peter followed the voice to an inquisitive blond man a few inches taller than he.

The man stepped up beside him and spoke before Peter could find words. "Hello, there," the man said. The words came out deeper than his previous statement, an obvious attempt at marking his territory as the alpha male.

"Troy Burkett," Hannah said, "this is Sheriff Peter Holbrook."

"Sheriff," Troy said with a nod, his gaze still wary.

The initial shock of Hannah being on a date wore off. "Nice to meet you," Peter said. He lifted his hand to Troy, who accepted it in a firm shake. "I've not seen you around Nowhere before. Your name's not local, either."

"My daughter and I just moved to Wichita a couple months ago," Troy said. "A bit of a change from the West Coast, but we're enjoying it so far."

"I see." Peter's voice mirrored his hesitance and jealousy, but he didn't care. "And, how did you happen to come across our lovely Hannah?"

Hannah shot him a look of warning mixed with curiosity. Peter ignored that as well. He knew he had no right to stake a claim on her now, but something about Troy's confidence challenged him.

"We were driving through town on the move to Wichita and stopped for a bite to eat at Hannah's diner. Hannah was so sweet and attentive to my daughter. Then again, she caught my eye as soon as I walked in. I could hardly believe it when she said she was single. I just had to take a chance and ask her out. Somehow I've managed to keep her around for a month now." He winked at Hannah. "This is what, our fifth date?"

"Wow, five whole dates, and it's not yet made the local newspaper," Peter said, allowing sarcasm to take control of his voice. "Of course, our Hannah's always been pretty good at keeping her love life details to herself."

"That's probably a good thing," Troy said with a smile, as if Peter had just complimented the couple on their longevity and handed over his blessing.

Peter shoved his hand in his pocket and pulled out his cell phone, eager for an excuse to escape. He fumbled with it for a moment, as if checking it. Glancing up at Hannah, he said, "Kaylen texted so I better think about heading out."

"Your girlfriend?" Troy asked, driving home once more that he was with Hannah.

"No, Troy, not my girlfriend," Peter said. Shifting his eyes to Hannah, he said, "Some of us are still waiting for that perfect girl." He nodded at them both. "Have a safe night."

Before they could respond, Peter headed to the bar. He picked up his lonely drink and plopped back down on the stool to finish it. An upbeat country love song filled the air, and Peter made the mistake of rotating his stool to check on Hannah. Troy stood beside her, his outstretched hand requesting a dance. She rose from her seat and, fingers laced with his, followed him onto the dance floor. Troy eased her into a steady two-step, Hannah's favorite dance. When Troy dipped her, she broke into laughter.

How did I not know?

Placing his hand on his chest, Troy mouthed the words to the song. Peter turned at Wade's scoffing behind the bar.

"That stuff don't really work on women, does it?" Wade asked.

From the smitten smile on Hannah's face, Peter concluded it worked too damned well.

"You know," Wade said, wiping a white towel across the top of the bar, "Mama says that sometimes what we want ain't for us to have. And, what we have, we don't always see."

Peter scratched his chin and swiveled on his barstool, facing away from the dance floor. "Your mama's a smart woman."

"Don't tell her that," Wade said with a laugh. "I'd have to start listening to what she tells me."

Peter set his half-empty beer on the counter and said goodnight to Wade. As he exited the bar, he resisted the urge to glance at Hannah. It was time for him to face forward and stop looking back.

Chapter Twenty-seven

While Peter's heart shattered in *The Hole*, the gray had taken over Nowhere, and it seemed to tighten its grip as he drove home. He twisted the volume knob on the car radio to drown out the rain, but the events of the night kept his shoulders knotted and both hands affixed to the steering wheel.

A few miles before the turnoff onto the dirt roads leading to his house, Peter forced his left hand off the wheel. He reached across his body to rub at his tense, right shoulder. He repeated the process with his other hand. Though it didn't stop stress from flowing through his muscles, the quick massage helped ease some of his turmoil. He stared blindly ahead at the oncoming dotted white line dividing the road, lost in his spiraling thoughts. As much as the thought of demons plagued him, and as much as he knew he had a far bigger problem than his non-existent love life, he couldn't detach Hannah from his mind.

He had no claim over her. Had no right to jealousy, love, or even lust. She had her own life to live, and he had never once taken a step to let her know how he felt. He had imagined they would one day fall in line together without any reason to believe so. As if love and all that came with it were a magical thing, something that happened instead of something for which he would have to work. He had slept through their love story, the one he had conjured in his mind. No, more like he was locked away in a coma, where he could hear everything, *feel* everything, but couldn't respond to any of it, despite his desperation to communicate. Over the course of nearly thirty years, they had played keep away with their hearts… and, tonight, he had won the game.

Standing on his front porch, the downpour of rain behind him, he slipped the house key into the lock and pushed open the farmhouse-red front door. He stepped onto the rug covering the foyer linoleum and scraped his boots across it.

"Peter?"

He ignored Kaylen's call as he took off his jacket and hung it on the coatrack's hook below his sheriff's hat. He shuffled down the hall, images of Hannah dancing with her date rolling through his mind.

At the entrance to his living room, Kaylen appeared. "Are you okay?"

The corner of his mouth tried lift in a greeting, but failed halfway up. He couldn't get Hannah's smile at that man (*Troy, his name is Troy*) out of his mind.

But, more than Hannah's smitten expression weighed on Peter as he ambled into the living room without clear direction or conviction. He stopped near the coffee table and stared off into nothing. Heard nothing. Felt nothing. Just another zombie with a broken heart.

From the corner of his eye, he noticed Kaylen lowering herself on to the couch. She scooted to the edge of the cushion, leaned over, and clasped her hands between her knees. Peter followed her lead and took a seat on the coffee table, facing her, but still speechless.

"Did something happen?" Kaylen asked.

Beads of rain flew off the ends of his hair as he shook his head. Other droplets raced down his face, tickled his neck, and soaked into his shirt.

Without a word, Kaylen disappeared from in front of him. Sounds of a drawer opening in the kitchen entered his ears, but he didn't give any thought to it. Within moments, she sat back down in front of him and handed him a dishtowel.

He accepted it and pressed the red cotton to his face. After it absorbed the dampness, he rubbed it over the hair on the top of his head with no real intention of drying off. He dropped the towel on the table next to him and folded his hands.

"Peter, I need to know if you're okay."

His eyes raised to hers, and her concern reached into his soul. "I'm a bit lost," he said, surprised at his admission. "Everything that's happened in the past few days – everything that's happened *tonight* – it's a lot to digest."

Small lines appeared around Kaylen's squinted eyes and downturned mouth. "I wish you didn't have to see it."

Though Peter knew she referred to her demon, he couldn't help but think of Hannah. His desperation to go back in time and not see Hannah with another man outweighed his desire to forget about Kaylen's demon. Did Kaylen know he had run into Hannah at The Hole? Did she sense the jealousy dripping from his sullied heart?

He had to ask himself, why did Hannah being on a date matter at all? Right in front of him, Kaylen waited for him to speak. An incredible woman who understood him. They connected on levels others would never imagine, let alone comprehend. For as long as he could remember, his life differed from all those around him, yet now he had met a woman like him. Someone who had just shown him her own inner demon, her most precious secret, the worst part of her. She trusted him that much.

"Do demons lie a lot?" he asked without thought.

"I'm sorry?"

"I've always heard they lie."

She collapsed into the couch. "They don't lie so much as they distort the truth. They take small truths and twist them, molding them until the truth is almost unrecognizable, but there is always some truth to that lie." Her tongue darted across her lower lip, and her face scrunched up. "Um… did it say something? My demon, that is."

Peter hesitated, but her eyes pleaded with him to be honest. "It said you think about me. A lot."

She smiled, a combination of relief and embarrassment. "Of course, I think about you. You're right here with me all the time, and I'm trying to help you."

"No, Kaylen," he said, his voice stronger and surer. "It said you *think* about me."

Though her smile remained in place, her eyes dropped, and she stared at her lap. "What else did it say?"

He took a moment to consider what he else he should tell her. "It said I think about you, too."

She sucked in a breath, but still didn't look at him. "Do you?"

Peter shifted his body sideways and scooted forward until his knee touched hers. He raised her chin until she lifted her eyes. "I think you already know the answer to that."

Their eyes locked in a tension-filled silence, during which they said so much. Spoke of things they wouldn't dare to say out loud, things they would never admit in the light of day. Those things they had both thought about, as the demon had said... all of it burst out of them in that silence.

Kaylen broke the gaze first with a jerk of her head as if something suddenly roused her from a deep trance. "I suppose I'd better get to bed," she said, her words timid and cautious. Her legs wobbled as she rose from the couch.

He inched up to a standing position and caught her arm before she could turn and run for the guest room. "I suppose so."

"Peter—"

His lips cut her off, but she didn't fight him. She didn't push him away or jump back in surprise, as he expected. Instead, she pressed into him, moved her frantic lips in time with his, and exchanged part of herself with him, those intimacies that they both desperately tried to hold back.

His fingers crawled through her hair, entangling themselves in the soft, midnight strands. He pulled her closer to him to explore her more, kiss her deeper, and let go of his own frustration and disappointment. Desire swelled inside him, consuming every thought and obliterating the world around them.

Kaylen broke away from him suddenly and caught her breath. "Peter... We can't... *I* can't..." She moistened her lips. "You know this isn't right."

"No," he said, his thumb caressing her cheek. "I don't know that."

For the first time since picking her up from the hospital, uncertainty flashed in her eyes, reverting her back to the timid, frightened girl without a memory.

"We... uh, we have to stay focused, Peter."

"I'm extremely focused," he said without hesitation.

He shifted his hand until his fingers touched her mouth, then trailed across her jawline and to the back of her neck. Her eyes closed and lips parted, inviting him in for another kiss. Her palpable fragility terrified him; just a couple hours earlier, she had been strong and forceful. In control. Now, she seemed to lay herself in his hands, ones that had no idea what to do with his attraction. Act on it, or remain silent, as he had with Hannah.

The thought spurred him into action, and he quickly claimed her mouth with his. As he fumbled with unbuttoning Kaylen's shirt, he thought about how he had waited so long for Hannah. All the wasted time and emotion. All the what-ifs and have-nots.

He wouldn't make that mistake again.

Chapter Twenty-eight

A soft glow from beyond the doors leading from his bedroom to the wraparound balcony caught Peter's attention as soon as he opened his eyes. He expected it to be dark, given that the clock on his bedside table proclaimed the time as six minutes past three in the morning. Six minutes into the witching hour, as he had once heard it called.

Kaylen stirred beside him. He rolled over to move closer to her, but a breeze blew through the room, seemingly coming from the balcony doors, which were not open. The light from the doors beckoned him, and he slipped out of bed. His feet glided toward the doors, his palms gripped the doorknobs, and he yanked open the glass panes. Sunlight blinded him for a moment, but he welcomed the warmth on his skin. When the sensation spread to his soul, it forced the corners of his mouth to turn upward.

Stepping onto the dark wood planks of the balcony, he moved to the railing and leaned against it. Butterflies layered his backyard, their colorful wings rippling like waves in front of a mass of oak trees in mid-bloom. All shapes and sizes of the insects floated in a chaotic dance with no choreography to follow, yet it all made sense somehow.

Laughter from behind him chilled him to the core. He swiveled around and faced the demon sitting on the edge of the bed, having escaped from inside of Kaylen. He jumped back at the sight, having only seen its face earlier. His limbs shook, but he tried to hold himself together and not show even the slightest hint of fear.

"Oh, this is brilliant," the demon said, folding its thin, misshapen arms and crossing its long, legs, ones that contained an *irregular bone structure underneath stretched, thin skin.*

"It's a dream," Peter said without a hint of doubt in his voice.

"No dream. See, you're over there, and your body is over here." The demon moved its grotesque, crooked index finger from Peter's current form to his sleeping body. Then it pointed to itself. "I'm right here, but she's over there, next to your body."

Peter's gaze fell on Kaylen again, sleeping next to him. "I don't... I don't understand."

"It seems the bit of magic she conjured up earlier may have had some side effects. Rather delightful ones, if you ask me."

Side effects? *Peter thought. Kaylen hadn't mentioned that anything might go wrong with the spell or that walking could have horrific consequences.*

"I see you're just as surprised as I," the demon said. "Although, I'm a bit more surprised to wake up in your bedroom with my vessel disrobed under your sheets. I was rooting for you two kids to get together, but what will Hannah say when she finds out?" Rows of sharp teeth emerged beneath the demon's smile. "Oh, that's right. She has someone keeping her company, too."

That the demon knew about Hannah unnerved him, and his question came out clipped. "How do you know that?"

It tapped a sharp fingernail against its temple. "I'm in your cantaloupe, Peter. I know everything now. Every little sordid detail of your mind-numbing life. Apparently, another side effect of your sorceress's feeble attempt at magic. You and I are now connected."

"No, we're not," Peter said. "This is a dream. Nothing more. I feared that something might go wrong, and now my mind is creating that in a nightmare. That's how you know about Hannah and Troy."

"Tell yourself whatever you need to, but deep down inside, where the squiggly things live, you know this is real."

Peter's jaw tightened, and his mind firmed up the idea of it all being a dream. But, a part of him believed the demon. A part he didn't want to acknowledge.

"There are days I wish I'd been created human," the demon said in almost a wistful tone.

Peter flinched.

"You get to experience so many things of which I'll never feel the full breadth. In other vessels before this one, I controlled the person entirely. Did what I wanted, when I wanted. But, it wasn't the

same as what humans feel. There's a filter between their skin and ours. Things like playing in someone's warm blood… well, I imagine it's not quite the same as if I were human."

Just as the ramifications of what the demon said hit Peter, it spoke again.

"Like what you did with this one tonight." It gestured toward Kaylen. "She doesn't often let me experience human pleasures. You'd think she'd let loose every now and then. Maybe kill someone. Even just a punch for fun. Maybe find a guy at a bar to play with. Drink something stronger than a beer. But, nope!"

Peter's eyes widened at the demon's sudden, high-pitched tone.

"All work and no play with that one. And, we all know how that affects a person." It swiveled its sunken-in eyes toward Kaylen. "Dull, dull, dull, dead."

In a flash, the demon stood in front of Peter, who jumped back and gasped.

"Will you kill her for me? Murder every now and then is oh-so good for the soul. You could feel her squishy parts between your fingers." It bared its teeth again and its voice splintered into multiple pitches. "And, when she's dead, you and I can play. I think we'd get along really well, Little Petey Holbrook."

Peter took several steps backward, until his back landed against his dresser. Realizing he had cornered himself, he side-stepped until he was in front of the balcony doors, which were still open. "What is it that you want?"

The demon circled in front of him, a lion sizing up its prey, its bones cracking with every step. "It's not about what I want. It's what all demons want. There's only one thing we chase."

Several seconds passed, but the demon did not emit its secrets. "What is that?" Peter asked, knowing the demon was baiting him.

It clucked its tongue, three times, with an agonizing silence between each one. "Don't want you thinking it's that easy."

Peter's belief that the encounter was a dream diminished. If it were a dream, the demon would answer all his questions. His own mind would make up the answers, and he'd have no way of knowing the truthfulness of the responses.

He reminded himself that he couldn't trust the demon even if it were here. He glanced at the bed, at Kaylen turning over on her side. A soft moan left her lips, and he wondered what dreams she encountered in the night. If the demon controlled her nightmares or if it really could leave her body while she slept. The tattoos were supposed to keep it in, but he supposed anything was possible in this world, the one that Kaylen brought to town with her.

"What are you doing, Peter?"

He looked up to see the demon had stopped pacing. "What do you mean?"

"Fred and Belinda are dead. So is Tanya. Keith has gone crazy. Lou Ann is probably dead by now. Your entire town is losing their minds or dying, and you're in bed with some woman you've known for a couple days. And, not even 'known her' known her. But, now you know her, dontcha, Peter? You know her in a real special way." It drew out the last few words.

"You make it sound like I'm a monster," Peter said.

"There are no real monsters, not in the true sense." The demon laughed. "Hell, not even in the figurative sense. Monsters are what you humans call people to make sense of it all. Like there's some bigger meaning behind bad things that happen. Maybe even evil beings, like demons."

"So, what? All people who do bad things are possessed?"

"No!" The demon grinned, its teeth glimmering under an unknown light source. "No, there are some very creative humans. The big ones, like Pol Pot, Hitler. The small-timers: Manson, Bundy. Lots of other names from the past. Lots more to come. There are so many of them that it makes me wonder if they were originally slated to be angels – fallen angels, that is – but ended up in the wrong production line."

Peter's stomach twisted at the conversation. If this weren't a dream – if the demon really stood in front of him – he had far better questions to ask. Things he had to know. "The butterflies… What do they do?"

"Why do you have to ask such ridiculous questions? They're harbingers. They foretell the most wonderful things to come."

"You mean death and destruction."

The demon shrugged its jagged bones where shoulders belonged. "Tomato, tomahto, crushed skulls. All the same to me. Especially if it's a redhead!"

Peter sucked in a deep breath and steeled himself against the demon's way of steering the conversation on to dark paths. He decided to get the discussion back on track. His dream – or whatever *it was – wouldn't last forever. "Why my town? Why me?"*

"Why don't you ask your little witch?"

Anger seared his veins. "Kaylen isn't a witch," he said through clenched teeth.

"Haven't you been paying attention in class? How do you think she has any abilities at all? She's not just a witch. She's a card-carrying, dues-paying High Priestess. The little protégé reached that level at the age of eleven. The only thing she doesn't have is a coven, which is where most power comes from."

"If she's as powerful as you say, why would she need a coven?"

"There's always more power. A coven can call upon what they think is Mother Earth or spirits or whatever the kids are calling it these days. But, they get a demon who supplies them with limited power at first, just enough to draw them in. Then, whatever the demon's agenda is, they can strategically increase that power. It's all about souls, Peter. And, production matters in The Below. If we have the numbers, we win the big war."

"The apocalypse? You and the others are trying to bring about the apocalypse?"

"Not so fast, cowboy. Don't start thinking your dot of a town – or your miniscule soul, for that matter – is apocalypse-important. That's some ego you have there."

Peter gave up on directly trying to get the demon to give up its plans for him and his town. He decided to ask another indirect question to lead it back to the topic. "Where do demons get their power? The Devil?"

"Limited from daddy-o. He's more of an overseer than a micromanager. Most of our powers are leftovers from the Great Fall of the angels."

"When you followed Lucifer into the pit of Hell."

"I love it when someone knows their history. But, souls… that's where the potent stuff lies. We possess a person or claim their soul, suck it down, and slowly feed on it. Tear it apart, piece by delectable piece. When it's ready to cast it off to The Below, we keep the power we've reaped. We just can't consume all of it, though. Gotta save something for The Below's funhouse."

"Feeding on souls. Sending them to Hell. There has to be more to it than that. Why else would you be here?"

The demon sighed with a raspy breath that sounded more like a wheeze. "I'm bored, Peter. I'm tired of answering your pathetic questions. *You think you can trick me into saying certain things because you think you're better than me. You think you don't deserve to be with me in The Below. But, you're just as bad as the rest of us. You're a murderer. And, we all know where murderers go.*"

"*I'm...*" Peter shook his head. "*I've never hurt anyone. I'm not a killer.*"

"*You are a murderer. You killed your mother.*"

"*My mot—*"

"*We all know it. She knows it. Seems you're the only one who won't admit it.*"

Peter's chest heaved with panicked breaths. "*I didn't kill—*"

"*You drove her to it,*" the demon said. "*Same thing as murder. She couldn't handle living with a freak of a son like you. With your epileptic jitters and your butterflies and your dying. She caught a glimpse of your future, and her disappointment in you stopped her heart from beating.*"

"*No, I didn't.*" Peter thought he shouted the words, but they came out muted and weak. He stared into the demon's eyes, and an instant calm came over him. "*I didn't kill my mother, but it doesn't matter what I say or do. Doesn't matter what I believe or know to be true. Same for everyone in the world. There will always be a demon there to make their beliefs real. To drag them further down that hole.*" He stepped forward, refusing to show weakness. "*You're that demon for me, aren't you?*"

"*I hope so, Little Petey Holbrook. In fact, I pray so. And, my father is much more powerful than yours.*"

Peter ignored the demon. "*What are you doing in my town?*"

"*I thought I told you I wasn't going to answer you.*"

An image of the door he saw when he walked flashed through his mind. "*Why do you want me to open the door? What's so important about it?*"

The demon's body appeared to tense. "*You'll never get the answers you seek. Not until it's too late.*"

"*Tell me what is so damned important about that door? Where does it lead?*" For once, the demon was silent, and Peter knew he was getting close. "*What is the door?*"

"*This isn't a game, Peter.*"

"*Then why do you keep playing one? Why don't you perform some more parlor tricks while you're at it? Make the furniture float*" around the room or fly out the window."

The demon paused and seemed to relax, as if gathering its resolve. "Your tone suggests you don't fear me. I realize I hold very little power in this realm, but that doesn't mean you don't have other things to fear. Others, like me, who are free to exert their powers in your world and decimate you with a snap of their fingers." The demon moved forward, and its feet lifted until it hovered over Peter. "You can't stop us, Peter. No one, not even the sleeping witch over there, can stop us."

"Seems to me you're not part of the collective, being trapped inside the 'sleeping witch.'"

The demon opened its mouth, defying human anatomy as it grew to the size of its head, showing every row of its teeth. For a moment, Peter worried it would devour him, but a piercing scream escaped the black tunnel at the back of its throat.

The sound blew Peter back until he hit the wall. He tried to lift his hands to his ears, but his muscles failed to work in the whirlwind of the scream. Desperate thoughts rushed through his mind, thoughts of waking up from his nightmare, returning to his world. Thoughts of holding Kaylen in his arms once more, of her body pressed into his, of her fervent kiss on his lips.

Something sucked at his midsection, painfully tugging and yanking. His spirit rushed back into his body, and his eyes flew open as he woke.

Chapter Twenty-nine

P eter stared at the relentless white of the bedroom ceiling as he adjusted to waking from his nightmare. Next to him, the empty bed swallowed his emotions like a black hole. She had been there while he slept, at least he thought she was. Unsure of when Kaylen had vacated her sleeping spot, Peter listened eagerly for some sound, some indication that she had not run away while he dealt with her demon.

Nothing.

He slipped out from the covers and swung his legs over the edge of the bed. When his bare feet touched the plush carpet, he bent over, his hand fumbling around for the boxer shorts and jeans he had ditched when they rushed into the bedroom with frenzied need the night before.

The denim came up over his legs, and he straightened up to button and zip them. His eyes searched for his T-shirt, but found it had disappeared. Maybe it was in the living room. Or, on the stairs. He couldn't be sure where in the house they had started disrobing.

A few steps away from the bed, Peter realized the doors leading to his balcony were ajar. His heart jumped as he recognized Kaylen had not fled his home like he anticipated. No, they had spent the night trading intimacies, and she remained in place, waiting for him.

Just beyond the glass doors, Kaylen leaned against the railing, his missing shirt masking the curves of her naked form. She did not turn around when he opened the door and stepped out onto the wood planks. Though he wanted to reach for her, he worried she might have regretted their night together. Instead, he stepped up to the railing beside her.

"It's beautiful out here," she said.

Peter followed her gaze over his land. The rising sun kissed the tops of the oak and pine trees and, through the leaves, projected shapes of nature across the dewy sprouts of spring green on the lawn. Kaylen's admiration of the morning reminded him of the simplicity of his life and abolished any lingering fears of his nightmare. He had always dreamed of moments like this with Hannah, ones that never came.

Maybe Kaylen had entered his life for more than one reason.

"I've traveled the world," she said. "Seen a lot of sunrises and sunsets, but never one so... calm."

He admired the oranges and reds for a moment, the same sky he drove under every morning on his way to the diner, but he never quite paid attention to it. Every now and then, a sunrise or sunset would stun him into silence, but having grown up in the area, the familiar sight became a blur. Just another part of his static daily routine.

He squinted his eyes and stared at the changing hues in the sky. "This isn't even one of the good ones," he commented. He twisted his head to look at Kaylen, who stared at him, eyes wide and mouth slightly open with surprise. "You should see the ones right after it rains."

"I don't know how you ever leave this balcony."

The longing in her bi-colored eyes captivated him. With her standing beside him, he was tempted to stay there forever. Ignore everything around them, the evil that penetrated his town, the demon that haunted his dreams. Forget about walking or spells or doors. In their bubble, nothing else existed.

Flashes of their night together knotted his stomach. He imagined she saw them, too, as her gaze flicked away from him and a soft blush embedded itself in her ivory cheeks. Unable to resist her any longer, he moved behind her and slipped his hands around her waist. Pressed against her with his arms wrapped around her and her hands clasped over his was the most natural thing he'd experienced in years.

A light kiss on the side of her neck elicited a shaky intake of breath from her. He looked out over his acreage again, content just to have her in his arms.

She lifted her hand off his and pointed. "Peter, look."

After a moment, he saw what she referenced. A single butterfly fluttered toward them until it settled on the railing of the balcony, just a few inches away from them.

His body tensed at the sight. "Something bad is happening."

Kaylen shook her head. "I don't think so. There are usually a lot more for that. I think this one is here for you."

He stared at the butterfly, took in every detail of the oranges and reds. Its eyes seemed to be looking back at him. "That's... impossible."

She twisted her head to the side and a smile consumed her face. "I think it's wonderful. Beautiful."

He released a hand from hers and pushed back her hair. His fingertips trailed over the side of her neck, his eyes traveling over the swirls of black etched into her skin. Pain lanced his heart at the thought of her as a child, enduring the tattoos. "You shouldn't have had to go through all this."

"It doesn't hurt anymore," Kaylen said. "The pain didn't last long."

"I don't mean that. You should have never gone through it in the first place."

"What were they supposed to do? I had a demon in me. Still do."

He aroused the nerve endings on her arm, tracing the symbols up to her jaw where they stopped. "Not this," he muttered. "They weren't supposed to do this. Not to you."

She rotated her body until she faced him. Though already squished between him and the balcony railing, Peter pulled her closer. His arms wrapped around her back, one hand wandering up her spine until it tangled in her hair.

"What we did... We shouldn't have done that," Kaylen said.

"Why not?" Peter asked, his lips hovering near her ear.

"I... I don't know." A small whimper escaped her as his lips brushed the skin on her neck. "I don't know that I care anymore."

Peter smiled and breathed in her scent. "I care," he said. Shifting his head to catch her eyes, he said, "Maybe a tad more than I should."

Her eyes lit up. "Me, too." Her palm conformed to his jawline and shook Peter's breath with her simple touch. "What are we doing, Peter?" The whispered question floated on the air between them, singing on the slight breeze blowing across the balcony, awaiting a response to guide them both through the unknown.

Peter's mouth opened, seemingly with promise of an answer, but words never emerged. His lips fell onto hers in a fierce, *hungry* kiss that provided everything he needed to know in that moment.

Chapter Thirty

"Thanks, Kirk." Peter disconnected the call with Detective Sergeant Kirk Carlson and looked at Kaylen. "Nothing back yet on the red paint on your car. He said to try back tomorrow."

Kaylen's shoulders lifted with a heavy sigh. "I wish I could remember more about the accident. I know it was a man who ran me off the road, and what I can see of his face seems familiar. Other than that, there's nothing."

Peter collapsed into the couch cushions next to her. "Do you think it's someone you've met since you've been in town, or someone you knew before?"

"I can't be sure."

He studied her face, the fine creases around her eyes, the pursed lips. On his usual day off work, they had spent half the morning in bed, distracting themselves by focusing on each other. Afterward, they went to work on figuring out who else in town could be possessed. On the coffee table was a list of suspects: those they knew were possessed and possible vessels for other demons.

Working on finding other demons distracted him every time his mind wandered to the nightmare. Spending time with Kaylen in the light of day reminded him that the demon couldn't leave her body. She had said the ink in the tattoos had a powerful binding spell, one that couldn't be broken. Not even by a demon desperate to join his clan on the outside. The night before had been nothing more than a nightmare brought on by walking for the first time. It couldn't possibly be anything else.

He hoped.

"Peter?"

Kaylen's voice jarred him out of his thoughts. He raised his head and found her staring at him. "Hmm?"

"You've been a bit lost in thought today." Her eyes narrowed, and she leaned forward. "Is it because we—"

"No," he said quickly. He wrapped his hand around hers and squeezed. "Not at all."

He brushed the back of his other hand against her cheek. Scooting closer to her, his palm conformed to her cheek, and his fingers gripped the back of her head. Their lips connected in a tender kiss. He didn't know what it was about this woman that made him want to ignore his responsibilities to the town, his friends... his life. To run away from everything and focus solely on her. Witch or not, she had certainly spelled him.

She broke away from him suddenly. A flush crept into her cheeks, and she lowered her head. "I can't... uh..." Her fingers flew to her lips, and she spoke through them. "We can't get distracted. *I* can't get distracted."

Guilt raced through his veins. "You're right," he said, regret creasing his brow. "I don't know..." He paused when he noticed the dampness in her eyes. Brushing her hair back from her face, he asked, "What is it?"

She lifted her head, and her gaze darted around the room. "I've really screwed this up. This damned amnesia thing. We've lost so much time to do this right. There are steps and procedures and proper ways to do this." She ticked off her fingers. "Investigate, identify, track, exorcise. It's the same every time, but here..." Her eyes locked onto his. "And, now with you—"

"Stop." His hand swallowed hers in a reassuring grip. "You didn't cause that car accident. You didn't bring these things to my town. You're here to help, and I need that. I need *you*."

A visible shift – a drive he had not seen before – in her eyes accompanied the straightening of her posture. A smile touched her lips for a brief moment, but dropped as she spoke. "You're right. But, I also need you to be honest with me about everything. Even if it seems insignificant, if you don't think it makes a difference, if you're embarrassed... doesn't matter."

Her words ripped the truth about his nightmare out of him. "I had a strange dream last night. About your demon." He waited for her to respond, but when she didn't speak, he continued. "It wasn't inside your body, and I felt like I did when I was walking. It seemed so real."

She leaned back and sighed. "Do you think it was a dream, or do you think it happened?"

"I don't know," he said. "I want it to be a dream, especially with the things it said. I thought it wasn't possible for it to leave your body, so it had to be a dream, right?"

"I've lived with this *thing* inside of me for well over a decade now, and I'm still learning things all the time. There's no precedence for having a demon trapped in your body by spelled tattoo markings."

She did nothing to ease his concerns about the nightmare. "Not exactly what I wanted to hear," he said.

"But, it can't leave my body, Peter. It is impossible. The only thing I can think of is if it somehow tethered itself to your consciousness when you walked. Then it followed you into your dreams." She threw her hands up. "I'm grasping here. I need to call Shane to find out if…" Her eyes widened. "Damn it!" She jumped off the couch and rushed toward the foyer.

Peter followed her to the front door, where she lowered her head and raised her hands, palms out toward the door. He started to ask her what she was doing, but stopped himself when he heard more low-toned foreign words coming from her.

"…*hinc patriam tutandam in aeternum.*"

As she spoke in the language he assumed was Latin, an orange glow appeared between her outstretched fingers. Peter stepped back as the same glow appeared etched in the trim around the front door, this time in the form of strange symbols, much like the ones inked into Kaylen's skin.

The symbols faded into the wood, as if they were never there, and Kaylen turned around. "A protective spell," she said. "One of the many things I should have done days ago. I need to do the same thing to all the doors and windows."

She brushed past him, leaving him in awe of what he had witnessed.

"*Kaylen isn't a witch.*"

"*Haven't you been paying attention in class?*"

His exchange with the demon in his nightmare hit him hard. This was the second time she performed a spell around him, the first being when he walked. She may have disavowed the coven in which she was raised, may have disconnected from her parents, may openly denounce the use of spells, but she seemed to have no issues using the knowledge and education her upbringing provided to fight demons.

He wondered about the cost to her. Did every spell damage her soul, as the demon suggested happened to those who dared to use magic? Or, was she immune from the consequences because of her work?

Lost in thought, he shuffled back into the living room and reclaimed his spot on the couch.

Within a few minutes, Kaylen returned, holding a picture frame in her hands. "Peter? Who is this?"

He rose from the couch and stood beside her. She held the photo up, one Shirley had taken of the deputies a couple years back. He kept it in his home office with the rest of his work.

"This man here." She pointed to the person three over from the left. "Who is this?"

His stomach churned with dread at the possible reason for her question. "That's Deputy Len Carter. He works at the station."

"He's also the man who ran me off the road."

"No," Peter said. "That's impossible. You met him at the inn the night your room was broken into. You must be remembering him from then."

"I remember him from the inn, but I also remember him from the accident. As soon as I saw that picture, it all rushed back." She closed her eyes as if focusing on her memory. "He pulled up next to me and tried swerving into my car, which is when I saw him. When that didn't work, he dropped back and hit me from behind."

The hairs on the back of Peter's neck bristled with her description of the cold manner in which one of his own, a trusted deputy and friend, ran her off the road.

"He was in a red car," she said, eyes still shut, "like a sports car. But not a new one; it looked older. It had this black stripe down the middle of the hood."

"He doesn't even drive a red…" He paused, the truth unraveling in his mind as he spoke. Len didn't own a red car, but his best friend and colleague, Deputy Doug Shultz did. A 1970 cranberry red Chevelle he had spent years restoring. He kept it in his garage, locked away for specific occasions, like a car show in Wichita or when he wanted to brag to friends.

A car that Len could easily borrow whenever he wanted.

"The car belongs to his friend Doug." Pulling his cell phone out of his front jeans pocket, he said, "I have to find out if Len borrowed his car. I can run by there and see if it's damaged—"

"You can't do that," she said. "You can't let anyone know about this. Len may be our only link to the demons."

"That's impossible, though." His mind whirred with rationalizations for the red car and Kaylen's recognition of Len. "Doug would have lost it if something happened to his car."

"Then, Doug might be one, too."

"No, that's not right. They've both been acting normal. They haven't gone crazy like the others."

"Not if the demon integrates properly with their soul. Only the ones who aren't strong enough who reject the demon go insane."

Peter scratched at the scruff running along his jaw. "There are hundreds of red cars in this county and the next one over. Thousands. Maybe…" He stopped when he caught sight Kaylen's sympathetic eyes and creased brow. "This… demon thing… it's taken so many people I care about already. I don't want to see anyone else hurt by it."

She moved in front of him and grasped his hand. Staring into his eyes, she said, "I'll do everything I can to stop them."

He pulled in a deep breath and exhaled slowly. "What do we need to do next?"

"This isn't a random demon infestation. It's too organized. We have to identify whoever is leading them. Once we drive that demon out, the others will follow. Demons are a lot like humans. There are leaders and there are followers. Kill the leader, and the followers disperse and are taken out one by one along the way."

"Quite a system you folks have set up for these things. How do we identify the leader?"

"Normally, I'd already have him or her identified. In this case, I'm about twenty steps behind, and the demons know I'm here. They'll do anything to stop me."

He nodded, already knowing what was coming next. "I have to walk again, don't I?"

"It's the quickest way."

"Let's do it," he said without hesitation. He dropped her hand and walked to the couch.

"It's safest to start at dusk." She shrugged and joined him on the couch. "These things have their timing in the world of the supernatural."

"I trust you," he said. Glancing at the clock, he realized they still had a few hours before the sun set. "Is there anything we can do in the meantime?"

"You can tell me every detail of your dream last night." Before he could protest, she said, "It's important that I know everything. Then, I can call Shane and fill him in. If this demon is somehow escaping me while I sleep or is connected to you because you walked, we need to know."

"Okay," he said, and proceeded to tell her about his encounter with the demon, leaving nothing out.

Chapter Thirty-one

A s the sun departed Nowhere for the night, Peter relaxed into the couch cushions the best he could. He folded his hands over his stomach and blew out all the breath from his lungs. "Why am I so nervous?"

Kaylen's face appeared over him. "Because you won't be dealing with just my demon tonight, but hopefully you'll find the leader of this tribe."

"I have a feeling this will never get easier."

"With any luck, this is the last time you'll have to walk."

"So, I find this head demon, and you go do your thing to exorcise it?"

"That's the plan," she said, with less confidence than her previous statements. "Last time, when you were in The Between, you were only in your house. This time, you're going out into the world. Everything you see happening is in this world in real time. But, you'll be viewing it from The Between. You can see people, but they can't see you. You won't be able to converse with or interfere with them."

"What about demons?"

"If you see a demon, stay away. They may not be able to see you, but they'll sense you."

What if they find me? Though the question lingered in his mind, he decided not to ask. He had to trust her and do his part to save his town. "I'm ready."

Her palms landed on each side of his face, and he closed his eyes. As soon as her thumbs touched his eyelids, they flew open, and her hands retreated from his face. "Are you okay?"

"I'm sorry," he said. "I just thought of something. I'm leaving the house this time. What if… Is it possible I won't find my way back?"

"Theoretically, anything is possible, but your soul is tethered to your body as long as you are alive."

"But, it's possible for me to lose my way. Is there something you can do… a spell or something that can make sure I find my way back?"

She leaned back in her chair, her gaze not leaving his face. "There is, but it could have its own ramifications."

"Anything as bad as my soul getting lost out there?"

"No," she said. "Nothing as bad as that. I can bind your soul to me as well. The effects may last for some time—"

"Do it," he said. "Please. I don't care about side effects as long as I can get back."

Her face remained stoic for a moment, then her head bobbed up and down. "Of course, Peter. I'll do it." She pushed her chair back and rose to her feet. "I'll be right back."

He rubbed his eyes and tried to calm his nerves while he waited for her to return. When she did, she had a steak knife and a dishtowel in her hands. He popped up to a sitting position. "What… what is that for?"

Sitting in the chair, she said, "A spell like this requires blood. Mine, not yours."

"No, I didn't mean for you to—"

"It's okay. It's only a little blood, and you're right. This is the second time you've walked that you know of, and we don't know how far you're traveling. I want you to easily find your way back. Plus, if we're bound together, I'll be able to feel if your soul is in distress and help pull you back to your body."

"What do I need to do?"

"Just sit there and face me." She placed the tip of the knife near the crook of her elbow and winced as she sliced into her skin. Blood pooled around the small cut, and she set the knife down on the table behind her. "Ready?"

When he nodded, she dipped the tips of her first two fingers into the blood. She then wet the tips of her fingers on her left hand and said, "Close your eyes."

He followed her instructions, and her hands wrapped around either side of his neck, her damp fingers touching the pressure points behind his ears.

"*Haec sanguinis vinculo.*"

She removed her hands, and they returned to his temples, her fingertips wet with fresh blood.

"*Haec sanguinis vinculo.*"

Again, her fingers left his skin. A moment later, two fingertips smeared blood on his lips.

"*Haec sanguinis vinculo.*"

He expected her to repeat the ritual again; instead, her mouth touched his with a sensual kiss. The metallic taste of her blood mixed in their intimate exchange, but it did not jar him away from her.

When she broke away from him, she whispered, "*Haec sanguinis vinculo.*"

His eyelids slowly cracked open to find her face still close to his. "Is it done?" he asked.

She nodded, and he grabbed the back of her head, pulling her back to him. He continued their kiss until he knew he wouldn't be satisfied with only that. He forced himself to stop and leaned his forehead against hers.

"Thank you for doing that," he said.

She quickly pecked his mouth again, then moved back. She used the towel to mop up the blood that had dripped down her arm, then wrapped the towel around it.

"I'm sorry I asked you to—"

"Don't worry about it," she said. She turned back toward him with a smile. "A lot of spells require a bit of blood to make them work."

Though his gut told him she was exaggerating for his sake, he didn't press her. He shifted to the side and laid back down on the couch. "Let's try this again," he said, closing his eyes.

Her hands returned to his face, as they were before. He tried to catch some of the Latin she spoke as her thumbs traced symbols over his eyelids, but he couldn't quite grasp her words. He realized his mind was instinctively fighting the spell, but he soon slipped away until the now-familiar feeling of his soul leaving his body came over him.

Sitting up on the couch, he took a moment to adjust to his surroundings. When Kaylen's demon appeared, showing only its face, Peter stood up and walked away. He heard it calling after him, but he remained resolved not to answer.

Leaving his home proved more difficult than he had imagined.

He couldn't clutch the doorknob in his spirit form. He tried to walk through the door, but his mind didn't want to accept the idea that he could pass through matter. He smothered the panic in his chest, and stared at the door. There *had* to be a way to pass through.

He told himself he was no longer burdened with physics, just as the demon had shown him with the floating furniture the last time he walked. Nothing prevented him from crossing to the other side except his preconceptions of a human not being able to walk through a door. Closing his eyes, he let the weight of his absent body leave his thoughts. He lifted his left foot, planted it down in front of him, and repeated the same with his right.

Several steps later, he opened his eyes to find himself on his front porch. Elation filled his soul at the sight. Fresh, night air bristled his spirit, a strange sensation he hadn't expected. Like a child in a wondrous new land, he marveled at the bluish hues over the land and the way his feet moved just above the ground. Not being able to take a breath, he missed the ability to breathe in the night, but he reveled instead in the new experience.

Once the newness wore off, he walked with determination across his front yard, but stopped at the street. He glanced left, then right, unsure of where to go. He had never asked Kaylen *how* to find the head demon, let alone any demons.

He reminded himself to stop overthinking things. He was no longer in his body, and, as with the door, he no longer needed to follow a rational course of action.

He closed his eyes once more and let the night settle over him. As soon as he stopped thinking, something tugged at his right side. Not a person, not a hand, but *something* – an intangible feeling that drew him in that direction.

His eyelids rose, and he followed the invisible pull. First, to the right. Then, after some time, left. Another right later down the road. Finally – miles after he began his walk – diagonal, through the trees lining the edge of Middle Park. When the trees thinned, he found himself on the south side of the clearing in the center of the mini-forest, one that many in Nowhere used as a secluded picnic area.

And, on the other side of the clearing, Hannah and Troy were doing just that.

Unsure of how close he could get to them, Peter stayed put. Whatever was guiding him had vanished. He was meant to be here, to see Hannah sprawled on her side across a large, blue blanket, Troy on his side facing her, both laughing and enjoying their time together. His gaze wandered to the bottle of wine tipped over. No liquid spilled out, and he imagined they had already consumed the contents.

He moved along the tree line, taking deliberate steps toward the couple, but stopped when he realized that, though hushed, he could hear them speaking. He turned his head and strained his ear toward them, until he remembered that he no longer had his normal senses. He wasn't sure how he could hear them, but it wasn't necessarily with his ears.

"This is so beautiful," he heard Hannah say. "We couldn't have picked a better night for this."

With his back toward Peter, Troy said, "I may have planned it that way."

"Oh, really?" Hannah said, laughing. "You planned for the sky to be so clear we can see every star?" She waved her hand toward the sky.

"Maybe not *that*," he said, joining in her laughter. "But, I may have had ulterior motives for bringing you here tonight."

Peter focused on the smirk on Hannah's face and the delight in her eyes. "What might those be?"

"I know we've been waiting," Troy said, "but I thought maybe tonight would be perfect. Special."

Peter's gut churned at where their date was heading. When Hannah moved closer to Troy and they stopped speaking, Peter turned around. It was a sick joke. It *had* to be. Why else would he be brought here to witness Hannah sleeping with her boyfriend for the first time?

Kaylen, he thought. He had no reason to be jealous of the scene at the park, not when he was sleeping with Kaylen. Not when he *cared* about Kaylen.

But, the part of him that had loved Hannah since they were children riddled him with pain.

"This town just keeps getting better and better."

Peter jumped at the voice and sudden presence beside him. His eyes widened as he recognized Kaylen's demon standing next to him and looking in the direction of Hannah and Troy.

"How did… What are… How are you here?"

"A blood binding spell," it said. "That's some pretty potent magic she worked back there. I, for one, am surprised she went through with it. Binding you two together… with blood, no less. That's not easy for anyone, especially the one casting the spell."

He ignored the demon and its continuing games. "What does that have to do with you?"

It snapped its head in Peter's direction. "It seems that binding spell connected more than just you and her. You and I might be friends for life now."

Peter shook his head. If the demon was bound to him, then maybe it was the thing that guided him to Hannah and Troy.

"Poor Kaylen," it said. "She's now bound to you and here you are, pining over the woman you really want. But, this one is getting to know the man she wants pretty well." It turned to him again and pointed toward Hannah and Troy. "Are you sure you don't want to watch? It's fascinating."

Peter sifted through the demon's words, but chose to not respond.

"Why don't I give you something else to focus on?" the demon asked.

A bright light flashed in his peripheral vision. Turning his head, he followed the glow to somewhere in the thick of the trees. Though he knew the demon was trying to trick him, the light drew him in with a pull as magnetic as whatever had brought him to the clearing.

Branches that he normally would push away passed through his spirit with ease. The density of the trees seemed to have increased since he first came through, and he walked much further into what he now considered a forest than before. His own rabbit hole to slide down, with the demon controlling every part of his environment.

When he came upon the source of the light, the small spot grew into a door – exactly like the one he had seen before. The one through which he wasn't supposed to walk. The one that called to him like a siren on the high seas lulling sailors to a vicious death. He glided toward it, unable to stop himself.

Don't open the door, Peter.

He heard Kaylen as if she stood next to him, and a tremble rocked his hand that hovered over the doorknob. He withdrew his hand, but stopped when the demon whispered over his shoulder.

"You can open it. You know it's the right thing to do. That's why you're so drawn to it." Its voice slithered through Peter's mind, choking out his every concern. He gripped the doorknob and twisted.

Peter, no!

Kaylen's voice ripped him out of his trance, and he jumped back from the door. He turned to the demon, who bared its teeth. Peter ignored the growl that came from deep inside it and said, "I won't do it."

"You will, Peter. You walk between doors. You can't help yourself. Might as well give in now and get it over with."

"No," he said. "I'm not playing your..." He paused when he realized he could no longer hear moaning or any other pleasurable sounds coming from Troy and Hannah. How long had he been in the forest with the door?

He ran past the demon, into the clearing. They had disappeared. Dread filled him at having lost track of the couple. He wasn't sure how he knew, but he was supposed to follow them when they left. And, now...

He whipped around and faced the demon, who stood right behind him. "You tricked me," he said. "You created that door to keep me away from them. How long ago did they leave?"

"I don't know what you're talking about," the demon said, its lips curving into a sneer.

"Where are they?" Peter shouted the question, but the demon seemed unfazed.

"I only wanted to spare you the sight of their passionate comingling." A jagged smile opened to reveal every row of its sharp teeth. "Now, it's our turn to play."

Chapter Thirty-two

At the sudden change in the demon's appearance, Peter stumbled and fell backward, his hands cushioning the impact of the dense ground. The demon's mouth widened, until it encompassed the entire surface of its face.

Peter scrambled away from the demon until his back hit a tree trunk. The demon bent over, its angry mouth closing in on him. Peter ducked to the side and screamed, "Stop!"

The demon shifted its body to face him again. "What do you mean, 'stop?' You have no say over what I do."

"And, you have no power in The Between." Peter didn't know where the strength to speak up came from, but it seemed to work.

The demon straightened up, and its mouth closed. "I have more power than you know."

Peter pushed himself up from the ground and brushed the dirt off his hands. "If you did, you would have killed me long before now." He stepped forward, closing the distance between himself and the demon. "But, the tattoos won't let you hurt me, will they? They take away most of your power."

"You're wrong," the demon said, backing away from Peter. "I choose not to use it against you. You're too much fun to play with."

"No, that's not it at all. In fact, I think you're a little scared of me. He Who Walks Between Doors. You need me, but I can do more than open that door for you, can't I?"

The demon vanished. Peter gasped in a breath, wondering if what he saw was real. He scanned the area, but saw no hint of

Kaylen's demon.

He twisted back around and looked at the spot where he had last seen Hannah and Troy. He raced across the clearing to the location and focused on the flattened patches of grass. There was something there... something he had to see. Something to follow.

A tug on his left side answered his unspoken questions, and he moved in that direction without another thought. As before, he let whatever it was direct him until he reached the small fishing lake just on the outskirts of town. In the parking lot, two figures exited a car. Troy and Hannah.

"What are we doing here?" Hannah asked.

"I have a surprise for you." Troy grasped her hand and led her toward the walking trails.

Peter followed them from a distance, but listened intently to every word.

"I have the early shift at the diner," Hannah said.

"I know it's late," Troy said, "but it's worth it. Trust me."

They continued with inconsequential conversation, as they branched off to the right at the trail's fork. They traveled further down the path, winding with it through the trees that surrounded the lake. Knowing they had wrapped around half the lake, Peter's curiosity about their destination grew.

"What's that?" Hannah asked.

Peter drifted to the side so he could see around them. He noticed an orangish-red glow, much like what Kaylen's spells created, but also similar to the door. Looking to the left of the glow, he spotted another one. Then, another.

"Part of the surprise," Troy said.

"It's curious, isn't it?" the demon asked, suddenly beside him.

Peter bristled at its voice. He had hoped the demon wouldn't show itself again.

"Where is he taking sweet, innocent Hannah?" The demon chortled. "Well, not so innocent anymore, is she now? Not after what I saw."

"Shut the hell up," Peter said.

"Your choice of words is sickeningly pun-filled."

Peter blocked out the demon again and rushed to catch up to where Troy and Hannah disappeared into the trees. He followed the lights to another small, treeless patch of ground. This time, instead of just Troy and Hannah, he found several of his townsfolk in the clearing. Three small fires were alight on the ground, circled by rocks. People he recognized, some of whom he'd shared meals and memories with. Some he'd known since childhood. Then, there were Len and Doug, two men he trusted as deputies to help protect his town.

And, all of them had demons peeking through their skin.

He ducked behind a tree, worried that the demons inside the people may see him. He looked around for Kaylen's demon, but it had disappeared without taunting him further.

"Troy, what is this?" Hannah asked, the first hint of anxiety threading her voice. "What are they all doing here?"

Len and Doug stepped forward, stopping when they reached Hannah. "It's an important night," Len said. "We wanted to be here to support you."

They each grabbed one of her arms and dragged her toward the others.

"Hannah!" Peter slapped his hand over his mouth as soon as her name crossed his lips.

Troy jerked around and scanned the area.

Peter hid behind the tree again, lowering himself to the ground in hopes of not being seen amongst the brush. He didn't know how to take on one demon, let alone the dozen or so that stood in the clearing.

"Troy, help me!"

Peter dared to peek around the tree trunk, and saw Troy had turned his attention back to Hannah.

The people crowded around Hannah, but Peter could still see her between bodies. She writhed in Len and Doug's grip, but could not break free.

"This won't take but a moment," Troy said. "Come forth, Babarithus."

A dark shadow comprised of some sort of mist, its shape constantly shifting, floated through the people and stopped in front of Hannah.

Hannah screamed for help, shattering what remained of Peter's heart. Her hoarse voice dissolved into a whimper when Troy's hand landed on her forehead.

"Babarithus, your time has come. Your name will echo in the halls of The Below for all eternity. *Intra autem, et consume!*"

The dark figure moved to Hannah and passed through her

body. Hannah's form shook with such violence that Peter thought she might be having a seizure. The jerking slowed as the demon melded with her soul.

And, then, she was no longer Hannah.

Something in her eyes shifted with a blink, her expression calmed, her limbs stopped flailing. Len and Doug released her, and a smile crossed her face.

Defeat encircled Peter and threatened to devour him. He pushed back and focused his thoughts on Kaylen. He had to get back to his body and help Kaylen stop Troy. Kaylen could rid Hannah of her demon and exorcise the demons from everyone. His town could return to normal.

But, first, he had to get return to his human state.

Crouched behind the tree and concealed from the others, he steadied himself and thought of nothing else but Kaylen and home. He could sense her with him, but didn't know how to reach her. How to let her know he needed her to whisk him back.

He froze at the sound of branches cracking and prayed it was only Kaylen's demon come back to torment him. He quickly realized her demon wasn't in human form; it couldn't break a branch any more than he could.

A strong voice stopped him from moving forward. "There you are, Sheriff," Troy said. "I thought I sensed you earlier."

Peter leapt to his feet to run, but Troy appeared in front of him. Peter stilled his movements, as he realized Troy looked everywhere around the tree, but seemed to look right through Peter.

"I know you're here," Troy said. "I may not be able to see you, but you're here. And, it won't take much to make you show yourself."

Though Peter couldn't feel his heart working in his spirit form, a phantom beating escalated inside of his chest. Something tugged at his midsection, lightly at first, but then stronger.

Still standing in front of Peter, Troy closed his eyes and held his hands up. "*Occultus autem se habet ultra spirit—*"

A black hole swallowed Peter as something dragged him backward through the air until he landed hard on an object. His couch. His eyes opened, and he flew off the couch, knocking Kaylen off her feet.

"Peter!"

He tried to apologize for bowling Kaylen down, tried to help her back up, but he couldn't manage to catch his breath or prevent his heart from raging against his ribcage. His compressed lungs fought against incoming air, despite desperately craving the lifesaving oxygen. Sputtering coughs racked his body, and his insides seemed tangled and torn, as if they had gone through a wood chipper. He had never experienced such helplessness. Every second ticked by like hours, framed by the deafening rhythm of his heart.

Kaylen helped him back onto the couch, and sat on the chair in front of him, her hands on his arms, her eyes intent on his. "Peter, calm down. Take slow breaths."

He focused on her and followed her cues until the panic attack and the pain from being whipped back into his body subsided. Slowly, surely, his heart returned to normal, and he could fill his lungs once more.

After a few moments of calm, Kaylen asked, "What happened?"

The panic returned, but Peter headed it off before it could consume him. "Hannah. There's… there's a demon in her." Every muscle tensed as he continued. "They put a demon in her."

"No," Kaylen whispered. "Who did it? Who summoned the demon?"

"Troy, her boyfriend. He already had one in him, and so did the others around him. People from our town. They were all…" He paused to find the right word. "Possessed. And, now she is, too." He frantically searched Kaylen's face for an answer. "Hannah is possessed."

"The evil in this town is greater than it's ever been. That man… Troy. He must have brought it here. Then, he inserted himself in a place of trust with Hannah to get to you." Kaylen shook her head and huffed. "We have to find Troy. What do you know about him?

"Nothing, really. He's not from here."

"So, you've met him before."

"Just once, briefly."

"That's okay," Kaylen said. "Tell me everything you remember."

He relayed his conversation with Hannah and Troy at The Hole the best he could recollect.

"A daughter?" Kaylen asked. Her lips pursed and face scrunched up with disbelief. "That's odd. Not that they wouldn't possess someone with kids, but a single parent? It's harder to hide when there's a child involved. They… see and sense things that adults can't."

"Could she be older and not know he's possessed? Like a teenager?"

"It's possible. Do you happen to get his last name?"

"It was something not from around here," Peter said, as he rooted through his memory of that night. "Birch, Burke… wait." He snapped his fingers. "Burkett."

Kaylen dug her cell phone out of her pocket and dialed a number. She held the phone up to her ear, but lowered the mouthpiece below her chin. "You said he's living in Wichita?"

"That's what he told me. He had just moved there."

"Shane," she said into the phone. "I need you to run someone down for me. Troy Burkett. Possibly in Wichita. Has a daughter." She paused for a moment. "No, I don't have her name." She glanced at Peter for confirmation.

He shook his head.

She spoke again into the phone, and he made his way into the guest bathroom. After cleaning Kaylen's blood off his skin, he headed into the kitchen. They had eaten all the leftover Chinese food from the evening before, but he still had a few beer bottles in the fridge. He grabbed one and closed the fridge door. He opened the bottle and went back into the living room, where Kaylen was still on the phone.

"That's not right. Are you sure?" She listened for a few seconds before scrambling for the notepad and pen on the coffee table that they had used earlier. "Okay, give me that address." She scribbled some notes, then put the pen down. "Thanks, Shane." She disconnected the call and accepted the open beer Peter offered. "We have an address to check out."

"That was fast," he said.

"Shane has his ways."

"If Troy is here in Nowhere, should we really take the time to travel to Wichita?"

"We aren't going to Wichita. The location Shane found is on the outskirts of Nowhere County. It's a farmhouse just over the Butler County line."

"He must have lied about where he lives, but that makes more sense than Wichita. He can come in and out of town easier."

"And, direct the demons under him to do what he wants." She lifted the beer bottle to her lips and swallowed several gulps. Her tongue ran across her lips, and she handed the bottle back to him. "Why don't you stay here? The house is warded against evil, and—"

"I'm not staying here and leaving you alone against those... those *things*."

"I've done this hundreds of times, Peter."

"Doesn't matter. I can't let you go to his house alone."

"Okay," she said. "We'll do this together."

Chapter Thirty-three

Sitting in his pickup truck half a mile down the dirt road from Troy's house, Peter reached into his glove compartment and retrieved his personal firearm, a Glock 17. He checked the magazine to ensure it was full, then pushed it into the gun. He stared at the gun for a moment and chambered a round.

"Sure you don't want more than a flashlight?" he asked, handing her one of the two they brought along.

Kaylen waved the flashlight at him. "I'm sure." She pointed it at the gun. "You know that won't do much good, right?"

"You say that," Peter said, "but I'd rather have it if we need it."

"Just, shoot for the limbs, okay? If you kill someone who is possessed, the demon can hop bodies. If you incapacitate them, I can still exorcise them."

"I can do that. Why come here, though, if we know Troy is in Nowhere?"

She stared ahead at the darkened road, toward Troy's house. "This feels like more than just a demon heavy-hitter and his merry band of followers invading a small town. He may have something in his house to help us understand what we're up against."

"Where do you suppose his kid is?"

"Not in that house with no lights on. If this guy is out with Hannah, like you saw, then his daughter is probably at a babysitter."

He nodded, but didn't say anything.

"It's okay if you're anxious," she said. "It's normal."

"Aren't you?"

"To a healthy level, I suppose. A little bit of fear keeps me alive."

"Then, maybe we'll both come out of this unscathed."

"That's the plan." Kaylen tugged on the passenger door handle. "Ready?"

He exited the truck in response and joined up with Kaylen at the front of the truck. Above them, the full moon and a mass of stars provided the only illumination. "Wish there were a few street lights," he said.

"I'm sure that's precisely the reason he picked this location."

They journeyed the rest of the way to the house in silence. Bits of gravel crunched beneath their shoes, but every so often, a patch of damp dirt from that morning's rain slurped up their soles, attempting to suck them into the ground. The sound drove Peter to the brink of wanting to run in the other direction, far away from demons and magic and realms between this world and the next, but he strode forward. Kaylen had done this possibly hundreds of times in the past. As with walking, he just needed to follow her lead. Trust her.

Several feet away from the house, she stopped. Peter waited with her as she sized up the area. No threats jumped out from behind the trees, no monsters moved inside the house, and no lights to guide demons through the halls.

"Something isn't right," Kaylen said, her head tilted back.

He followed her gaze to the sky. Gray consumed the night, not allowing a single star to shine through. He turned around, ensuring the dirt road had not disappeared, and he jogged back to it. From there, the stars existed as they always had. They hung in the same places he and Kaylen had left them when they stepped onto Troy's property.

He resumed his position next to Kaylen. No stars.

"I don't know much about the country life," Kaylen said, "but I'd say that's not normal."

"It's the gray," he said. "The clouds should be covering the stars up from every direction, but it's only right here."

"I've never seen this happen before."

His ingrained fear of the gray – starting as a child in the hospital – rushed through his veins and a lost memory returned. After he'd had the seizure as a child, the one that claimed his life and gave him the gift of walking, he had watched the gray from his hospital room window. He sensed the demons hidden within the storms… he might have even seen one that night. The gray was definitely a test from God, as his mother always said, just so much more than he could have ever imagined.

"Somehow, the gray is connected to the demons," he said, "but it's like the gray is centralized here, over this house."

"Makes sense since this guy is possessed by the demon in charge. How often did you say the gray comes?"

"Every year around this time."

"Then, the demons are coming here year after year, bringing the gray with them, and searching for the perfect time."

"The perfect time for what?"

She flicked her flashlight on and held the beam toward the ground. "Let's go find out."

They walked side-by-side up the brick path to the front porch. When they reached the front door, Kaylen asked, "Are you going to be okay with me breaking in, or do you need to look the other way?"

"Lucky for you, I'm off-duty and this county isn't my jurisdiction," he said with a sarcastic undertone. "Besides, no extreme measures needed to break in."

She shot him a curious glance.

"You really don't know anything about country life." He twisted the doorknob, and the door creaked open. "No one locks their doors out here."

"Makes my job easier," she said, taking the lead and walking inside.

While Kaylen explored the large foyer, Peter's flashlight beam danced around the living room. Dust coated a broken, antique couch, its flower-covered upholstery ripped and torn with age. His light flashed on an old bookshelf lined with musty porcelain dolls, some missing limbs and eyes, and cracks running through their once-adored faces. A cobwebbed radio that looked like it hadn't been used in over half a century sat on a cart where a television would normally be.

Peter lifted a hand to his nose to block out the musty odors penetrating the room.

"What is this place?" he asked Kaylen, as she joined him in the living room.

"A tomb," she said. "No one lives here. No one human, at least."

"But, the daughter—"

"Shh!" She held up her hand and froze in place.

Peter's eyes darted around the room as he listened for the slightest movement. A soft clicking from the far corner behind the couch caught his attention, but when he flashed his light at the sound, the area was empty.

He swung the light to the other side of the room, landing on the dolls. He hadn't studied them much when he first saw them, but he swore their positions on the shelf had changed. Goosebumps prickled the skin on his arms. He never had thought much about dolls before, never considered them terrifying, but something about these chilled him to the core.

One caught his attention, and he walked toward the shelf, his flashlight trained on the doll with a ripped plaid dress. Its right arm and left eye were missing. A deep crevice ran from its right eye, across faded freckles, and down to its smiling mouth. One of its smooth braids lay over its right shoulder; the other, a tangled mess, as if an angry child had taken a comb to it.

He whipped around at a sound behind him, and saw Kaylen holding up an end table she had bumped into. He smiled and nodded at her when she looked at him, and then turned back around to the look at the doll.

It was missing from the shelf.

The doll had been there a moment earlier. Only a few seconds had passed since he last saw it. But, in its wake, a doll-sized void in the thick layer of dust.

"What is it?" Kaylen whispered in his direction.

"I don't..." He shook his head, unable to explain the craziness he may or may not have witnessed. It had to be a trick of his mind. Maybe the doll had never been there.

The clicking grew louder. Whereas before it sounded like it came from the corner, the noise now seemed to surround them.

"What is that?" Peter asked, keeping his voice down.

"Spiders."

And, then, he heard it. The clicking legs of hundreds – possibly thousands – of spiders crawling over each other, making their way closer to the center of the room. To them.

"They aren't real," she said. "They're in your mind."

"The spiders are in both of our minds?" The sound retreated, as if his words scared the spiders away. He hoped it also stopped the dolls from playing with him.

"Something's screwing with us." She flashed her light in the corner of the room from where the sound came. "You know, I'm the first to admit when I'm wrong. We should leave."

The strange smell rolled through the air around him. He sniffed, his nose wrinkling at the decay in the odor. "Do you smell that?"

She pulled in a deep breath through her nose, and her eyes widened. "Sulfur. Peter—"

The attack came from above. Kaylen fell to the ground under the weight of the attacker, who Peter quickly realized was the missing daughter. The girl clawed at Kaylen, her thin arms swinging with a viciousness and strength of which they didn't seem capable.

Dropping his flashlight, Peter raced up behind the girl and dragged her off Kaylen. The child jumped about, trying to escape his grasp like an untamed, rabid animal. He tightened his grip around her shoulders and leaned back to help with his leverage on her.

Kaylen rose to her feet, blood dripping from cuts on her face. "Keep hold of it!"

He caught the use of "it" instead of "her," but with the girl flailing about, he didn't have time to consider Kaylen's word choice. "Doing my best here," he said. He pulled his head back as the girl attempted to ram the back of her head into his face.

Kaylen's eyes closed, and she lifted her hands, with palms facing up. "*Regna terrae, cantata Deo...*"

The girl struggled more than before, her strength increasing as she tried to break free.

"*...omni infernalium spirituum...*"

"No!" the girl shouted, followed by an elongated scream that sounded the same as the one Kaylen's demon had emitted.

Peter's eyes sealed shut, and he grimaced against the scream, wishing he could somehow block the sound out as well. The girl continued squirming in his grip, but with less power than before.

Continuing her Latin, Kaylen's eyelids slowly lifted, revealing an orange glow surrounding her bi-colored eyes. She spoke louder with each sentence, and the same orangish light floated in the middle of her palms.

The girl slowed her fight and relaxed in Peter's grip. Her head twisted to look back at him. Between her size and face, he estimated her to be eleven years old.

"She's killing me," the girl said in an innocent tone. "When she exorcises the demon, the spell will kill me."

Peter faltered in holding the girl. His lips parted, but no words emerged.

"Don't let her kill me," the girl said.

He lifted his gaze to Kaylen, who was caught up in the power of the exorcism spell. She didn't seem to notice the girl talking to him.

"I don't want to die," the girl continued, tears slipping down the one cheek he could see. "I'm too young to die."

"Kaylen," he said, quiet at first, then louder. When her eyes met his, he said, "You have to stop. You're hurting the girl."

As if she didn't hear him, Kaylen gave him no response, but continued with her spell through clenched teeth.

"Don't let her kill me!" the girl cried out. "You're the sheriff. Aren't sheriffs supposed to help little girls in trouble?"

Peter's concerned expression dropped, and a chill ran through his body. He wasn't in his uniform, and they had driven to the house in his pickup truck, so there was no way she would know he was the sheriff. Even if she did, she would have called him a policeman, like most kids did before they could differentiate between a policeman and a sheriff.

He immediately tightened his grip on the girl. The warnings Kaylen had given him about not talking to demons rushed through his mind. He had not listened to her; he had engaged her demon – whether real or imagined – in multiple conversations. Now, this demon inhabiting the girl's body was doing the same, dragging him into a farce so he would let her go.

"You're not a little girl," he said. He repeated the phrase under his breath several times, until his brain accepted the fact that he held onto a demon-possessed body.

"And, you aren't a sheriff. Not really." An inhuman cackle came from the girl. "Little Petey Holbrook and his epileptic jitters."

He jerked the girl back, hoping to shut her up. She repeated her little saying, the same one he heard all through his childhood. Everything that had built up over the years, all the anger he had ever held back, seethed from his pores. His muscles tensed, holding her a bit too tight.

The first snap entered his ears almost unnoticed. The second one he not only heard but felt beneath his right forearm. He froze, then loosened his grip on the girl. Did he break her arm?

Peter let go of her and stepped back. The girl's forearm folded in half, and bone stuck out from the skin.

"What the hell?" He couldn't tear his gaze away as another several snaps came from inside the girl's body.

"You aren't getting off that easy," Kaylen said to the girl, followed by more Latin.

The girl's body and limbs twisted and contorted in unnatural positions, while bones continued breaking. A strange crunching sound followed, as if her broken bones were being ground into dust.

"...*ipse fortitudinem plebe Suae!*"

With Kaylen's shout, the girl dropped to the ground in a pile of skin and bones that no longer resembled a human body. Peter inched forward, drawn in by the mutated mess.

In front of him, Kaylen collapsed to the floor. He ignored the girl's corpse and ran to Kaylen. "Are you—"

"I'm fine," she said, waving him off. "I just need a moment." Lifting her head, she added, "One too many spells today."

"You're bleeding," he said. He raised his arm and used his sleeve to wipe away several drops of blood under her nose and from the superficial cuts on her face. "What can I do?"

"I'm fine, really." She pushed herself up, and he helped her to her feet.

Looking back where the girl's body lay, he asked, "Did she die because of the exorcism?"

"No." Kaylen walked over to the girl and sighed as she stared down at the body. "There hasn't been a human soul in this body for a while. Weeks, maybe months. The demon killed this girl long before we found her." Heading for the front door, she said, "We're not going to find anything here, and I don't want to be around if more of them come here."

"Should we go to the park where I saw Troy last?"

"I doubt they're still there. Let's go to your house for a bit. I need to regroup my thoughts."

He internalized his thoughts for most of the walk back to the truck, but the tension coming from Kaylen more than bothered him; it scared him. With her experience, he assumed she would be more collected than she was.

When they reached the truck, he grasped her arm and turned her around. "I don't want to pry, but you don't seem okay."

Her head lowered, and her gaze dropped to their feet. "It's

been a long time since I've had to exorcise a demon from a child. Even though the girl's soul had moved on, it's still hard to see. This girl... she was what, eleven? Twelve?"

"About that."

"It's hard not to relate." She looked up, her pain apparent in the creases on her face. "That could have been me. My demon could have killed me if it had not been contained."

Peter had no response, no words of comfort to send her way. Instead, he pulled her into his arms, kissed her forehead, and held her until he could no longer hear the girl's voice in his mind.

Chapter Thirty-four

The gray had consumed Nowhere in the time they were battling the child demon. Peter pulled his truck into his driveway, as close to the front door as he could. The downpour pelted he and Kaylen as they raced inside the house.

"I'll grab some towels," he said when they walked inside. "Unless you'd rather change clothes. That rain can really soak you through to the bone."

"A towel is fine," she said.

He went into the laundry room and retrieved two fresh towels from the dryer. After they had mostly dried off, he asked, "Now what do we do? How do we find them?"

"That's where more time would come in handy," Kaylen said. "But, I have a feeling we're running low on that. There's something more to this than what I'm seeing. There was nothing normal about that child." She slumped down onto the couch, her shoulders hunched over, and put her face in her hands.

He sat next to her and placed his hand on her shoulder. "The spells you've done. They're hurting you, aren't they? It's not good magic, is it?

"There's no such thing as 'good' or 'white' magic. It's all dark, Peter. It's all a tool of the Devil. He tricks people into thinking that there are ways to use magic or power that is good, but in the end, it's all selfish. It's all is for their own gain. People dabble in witchcraft or play with a Ouija board. They think it's okay because the board is made by a toy company and says, 'For entertainment purposes only' on the package. It doesn't matter. It's still a form of witchcraft."

"The Devil uses whatever he can to entice people to him."

"Yes. Say 'Bloody Mary' three times into a mirror. Most kids think it's a parlor trick for slumber parties. But, if someone believes she's there, she will appear. The Devil makes sure of it. Then, there's television shows that portray Lucifer as a benevolent, caring, misunderstood guy. That's not the way it works. That's not the way any of this works."

"So, if all magic is dark, why do you use it?"

"It may be dark, but it's necessary sometimes. I can do it because of my demon, but I never overuse it. Magic always leads somewhere bad."

Peter decided not to press the issue. He hated that Kaylen used magic with him, especially if it could harm her, but she had hunted demons for so long that he had imagined she knew how best to handle it.

"Cattle mutilations," she said under her breath.

He raised his head at the sudden change in conversation. "What?"

"Cattle mutilations are a sign of demon infestation, but also of something else." Before he could inquire further, she asked, "Have you heard of Stull, Kansas?"

"Sure, there are legends about Stull. Every kid who grows up in Kansas knows about it. The cemetery up there allegedly houses a gate to hell."

"Except it's not real. It was a random story in the University of Kansas newspaper about legends dating back to the 1800s, and from there, it grew into an out-of-control myth."

"Most folks already know that or they learn it the hard way by going up there," Peter said. "Why bring it up if it's not real?"

"Because legends are never far from the truth. The Devil won't lead people directly to his lair. He'll trick them, take them around the block a few times. Sure, he'll steal the souls of those led astray by legends. He always uses tricks like that to bring in new flesh."

"So, Stull isn't a gate to hell, but a legend to lead people in the wrong direction. There are gates to hell elsewhere, though?"

"'Gate' isn't even the right word. More like 'portal.'"

"Which isn't in Stull," he said, a question in his tone.

Her eyes gave away the rest.

"It's here, isn't it? In Nowhere."

"With the activity in your town, I believe it is, and the demon in Troy knows that. Whenever a demon comes to our world, they want to bring others over as well, but nothing makes it easier than finding a portal. It allows mass amounts of their kind into this world. However, they need a guide to help open the portal, and guides aren't that common. It takes a long time to find a guide, so they have to be patient."

"I'm a guide, aren't I? He Who Walks Between Doors."

"You are, and I think you developed that ability with the seizure that killed you as a child. There are also seasons to these things. The portal can't be opened at just any time."

"I suppose now is the right time."

"The third day of the third month of the year, at three a.m." She glanced at her watch. "It's 1:30 a.m. on March third. It's also the first night of the full moon, isn't it?"

Peter thought for a moment, then nodded. "Yes, it is the first night of the full moon. Why those particular dates and times?"

"It's an inversion of three p.m., the hour Jesus was crucified and died on the cross. These are perfect conditions to open a portal to hell. They can be stopped, but we have to find the portal. Do you have a map of the area? And, I need a marker, too."

"Both are up in my office." He took the stairs two at a time and grabbed a map of Nowhere from his desk drawer and a black marker from his pen holder.

Back downstairs with Kaylen, they went into the kitchen, where he spread the map out across the table. "Where do we start looking?" he asked.

"Mark each of the spots on the map where deaths have occurred recently. Including the child tonight."

He carefully followed the roads on the map until he found each spot where someone had perished. He looked down at the four black dots, then remembered the cattle deaths and marked that as well. "I think that's it."

"What represents each of these spots?" She pointed to the one on the far left of the map.

"Fred and Belinda's baby died."

"Sacrifice of Innocence." Moving clockwise to the next mark, she asked, "What's this one?"

"Belinda murdered Fred."

"Sacrifice of Love." Her finger traveled to the next point.

"The cattle were mutilated."

"Sacrifice of Sustenance." At the next spot, she asked, "And, here?"

"Tanya killed herself."

"Sacrifice of Self. So, this fifth one," she pointed to the last black dot, "is where the possessed child died. Sacrifice of Youth." She looked at Peter. "Do you see the pattern?"

He stared at the map, desperate to see what she did. "The location of each incident on the map creates a circle."

Kaylen nodded, closed her eyes, and placed her open palm above the map. "*Illustrant semita.*"

An orangish-yellow glow, resembling fire, replaced the points. A circle emerged in the same light, connecting each circle. Then, other lines formed, connecting each of the dots diagonally, until a pentagram became visible.

He stepped back, as she closed her palm and opened her eyes.

"A pentagram," he said.

"No," she said. "A pentagram itself has nothing to do with Satan. But, look at the map again. This is north," she said, pointing to the top of the map. "The sacrifices form an upside-down pentagram. That's the symbol used for evil."

Peter walked around to her side and looked at the map from her angle, a chill flooding him as he stared at the upside-down pentagram.

She raised her hand again, opened it up over the map, and closed her eyes. "*Illustrant centro.*"

In the center of the symbol, an orange glow burned into the paper. When she opened her eyes, she gestured toward it. "That's the location of the portal and where the final sacrifice will take place."

Though terrified of her answer, he asked the question. "What's the final sacrifice?"

"Sacrifice of Demon. One of their own offers itself up as a sacrifice, then they use the blood of the vessel to open the portal."

"Hannah," he said.

"From what you described, yes. The demon has to volunteer itself for a sacrifice." She slid her hand into his. "I'm sorry, Peter, but I'll do everything I can to stop them before that happens. Do you know this place?" She pointed to the center of the upside-down pentagram.

After studying the map for a moment, he said, "That's behind the old Hickman farm. There are several outbuildings there. A couple barns, some storage buildings. They have well over one-hundred acres, so there's lots of privacy."

"Sounds like a great place for a portal. You realize that I shouldn't bring you with me."

"I'm going," he said, with no intention of backing down.

"The place will be littered with demons. Besides, bringing a guide to a portal is insane. More than insane. It's—"

"I don't care. I'm not letting you go alone, and people I care about are there."

"I didn't say I wasn't going to take you. I just shouldn't. It usually takes a few hunters to close a portal, but I don't have time to call in reinforcements." She moved in front of him and grabbed both his hands. "You have to do what I tell you, no questions. I will take the lead."

"Of course."

"And, no matter what, do not open any doors."

"You mean the door to the other side? Of course not. I'd never dream of—"

"You'd be surprised how easily they can sway someone into doing something they'd normally never do. They are capable of so much, and they have Hannah. I need you to stay clear-headed for me and do not open any doors. I've seen what happens if a portal is opened."

The severity of her tone concerned him. What would the demons do to try to get him to open the portal? They already planned on sacrificing Hannah. How much worse could it get?

He did not want to find out.

"I promise you," he said, "I won't open any doors, no matter what."

"Thank you." She touched her lips to his in a gentle kiss. When she broke away, she said, "We better get going. We have a long night ahead."

Chapter Thirty-five

A yawn controlled Peter's mouth, but his mind had never been more alert. Once his mouth closed, he shook his head, fixed both hands on the steering wheel, and adjusted his position in the seat. Adrenaline mixed with fear created a stew of anxiousness bubbling inside of him.

Glancing at Kaylen next to him, she seemed more focused than ever. Introverted, determined, all her emotions the exact opposite of his. He reminded himself she had done this before, but he still worried. There was a strange frailty about her, as if she had aged in the past several hours. Maybe it was too many spells in a short period of time, as she had commented earlier. Maybe it was the idea of facing a portal without her colleagues beside her.

He silently prayed they were strong enough together to save his town. To save Hannah.

Driving down the back, dirt roads across the Hickmans' property, guided by solar post lights along the path, the sky identified the location of the portal. A vortex of the gray swirled above one of the barns, lightning branching out between the dark clouds, providing illumination on the ground alongside more post lights.

He braked a few hundred feet away from the barn and switched off the engine. Kaylen didn't speak as she exited the truck. Gun in hand, he met her at the front of the truck and stared up at the full force of the gray.

"Are you sure you're okay to do this?" he asked.

"Are you sure *you're* okay to do this?" she asked, slipping her hand into his.

He opened his mouth to answer, but stopped. A butterfly

fluttered in his peripheral vision, and he turned his attention to it. As its wings flapped a few inches from his face, he looked to the right and noticed it had brought an army with it. Hundreds – possibly thousands – of butterflies lit up the field to their right. Though they didn't come as close as their leader, the sight reminded him that he wasn't alone. *They* weren't alone.

As a child, his mother had said he was destined for something great, and this was it. This was everything she had ever rambled about that had made no sense back then. This was what she had been institutionalized for. Died for. He couldn't let her down now.

"I'm okay," he said. He smiled at the butterfly in front of him, *his* butterfly, and strength surged through his veins. He looked at Kaylen and squeezed her hand. "Let's do this."

She let go of his hand and treaded forward, toward the barn. Peter matched her steps, and the butterfly flew beside them.

When they reached the outbuilding next to the barn, a rustling from behind the building stopped him from walking further. "What is that?" he asked Kaylen, who had also paused.

She closed her eyes and placed her hands palms down in front of her, as if steadying herself. After a moment, she said, "Demons. A lot of them." Opening her eyes, she looked at Peter. "They know we're here."

Within seconds, townsfolk appeared from between the buildings and from behind trees in the field, and walked around his truck. He recognized several of them immediately. Jim, Tanner, Luther, Stacy. But, seeing Shirley from the station caught him off-guard. As he watched his friends and citizens emerge from the darkness, he moved closer to Kaylen, his arm wrapping around her as protection.

"I need a little room for this," she said, with no ill-will in her tone.

He stepped back a few feet, but kept scanning around him at the encroaching demon-possessed people.

Kaylen raised her cupped hands in front of her, bowed her head, and closed her eyes, as if praying. At first, her words were muffled. Peter strained to hear while keeping on edge about the demons inching closer.

"*Dolores inferni circumdederunt me adhuc videor superis qui in me in virtute.*"

Her soft statement froze Peter. A glance in her direction

rendered a glimpse of white light in her eyes.

"I call upon the powers above to still my soul as I draw on the power of the one inside me," she said.

Her voice filled his ears, yet the people around them did not seem to notice anything. Not her chant, not the blinding white that had taken over her eyes, not the orange glow forming over her hands.

"...*superis qui in me in virtute.*"

Though spoken under her breath, he could clearly hear every word, as he witnessed her metamorphosis into something supernatural, driven by the power of something else. *Her demon.*

Repeating the phrase in Latin, her normally low tone grew husky and guttural. A translucent orb encapsulated her like a force field. "*In nomine Iesu Christi eieci te de hoc mundo.* I banish you from this world. *Et abiit.*"

Relying on his instincts, Peter ducked, but kept his eyes on her movements. Her hands shot out, and lightning branched from her fingertips. The orangish-red blaze seared each person, each demon. Like a mystical Taser, the electricity held them for a moment before they all dropped to the ground.

Kaylen fell to her knees and slumped over. Peter jumped up, but before he could race to her, she raised her head and spoke. "Go," she said. Blood painted her eyes like the stained glass in a condemned church, and crimson tears washed her ashen cheeks. "You have to go stop him. I have to exorcise these demons before they're back up."

Her enervated voice concerned him, but he had to find Troy. Until they eliminated him, no one would be safe.

Peter rushed to the barn without a thought for his own well-being. He slid open the door on the right, letting out a cloud of decay. The foul odor overwhelmed him, but he pushed through the intense scent of sulfur mixed with death. His gaze darted about the open space, from stacks of hay, to farm tools hanging on the far back wall, to an old, rusty tractor in the middle of the space that probably hadn't run in years.

"Sheriff." The man's voice came from the center of the barn seconds before Troy appeared from out behind the tractor. He waved his hand, and Peter's gun flew out of his grip and across the barn. "Glad you could join us."

"Where's Hannah?" Peter asked.

"She's at the portal, waiting for her time to come." Troy said.

"Would you like to see it?"

Against his better judgment, Peter raced past Troy. As he had said, Hannah stood looking down at an area where the wood floor had been hacked up and removed. Debris surrounded a hole approximately three feet in diameter. Peter walked to the edge and realized it was only a few feet deep.

"That's a portal to hell?" Peter asked. He had expected something more spectacular, supernatural.

"It doesn't look like much now," Troy said, "but when her blood runs into it, the ground will transform into the gate. Of course, then I'll need you."

"I won't open the door."

"Yes, you will, and it won't be very difficult to make you." Troy gestured to Hannah. "Come, my dear."

She lifted her head for the first time. Not a single muscle on her face twitched or tightened. A plastic smile remained stationary as her feet moved in Troy's direction. When she reached him, his fingertips brushed her jaw.

"You see, I can do anything I want, and she won't protest." He wrapped his arm around her and coaxed her to turn around, her eyes fixated on Peter. Troy's hand climbed her torso, fingers spread wide to receive her neck in his grip. "She won't defend herself."

The muscles in Troy's hand contracted, veins popping as he squeezed her neck. Hannah's smile barely budged, even with her gasps for air. She seemed to enjoy tasting death.

It's not Hannah, Peter reminded himself, but the thought didn't stop him from demanding Troy stopped. "She isn't a part of this! Let her go!"

Troy dropped his hand away from her neck. "Open the door."

Staring at the woman he grew up with – the woman he'd loved since before he could even define the emotion – Peter didn't recognize her. She had the same auburn hair, the same wide, green eyes, the same freckles on her nose and cheeks that he teased her about. But, it wasn't Hannah. He could no longer see her soul in her eyes.

"She's not in there," he said. "She's already gone. That's just a shell."

"I can see how you would like to think that," Troy said. "It's easier to rationalize disobeying me if you believe you have nothing to lose. Your Hannah is in there."

"Show me." Peter imagined that at any moment, Troy would snap his fingers and obliterate everyone in the room. But, if Peter were to give into the demands, he had to know that his Hannah was imprisoned in her body.

Troy eyed him for a few seconds before turning his gaze to Hannah. "Go." He flung his hand in Peter's direction.

Her slow, deliberate steps, feet crossing in front of each other like a seductress, stuttered halfway to him. A crease formed on her forehead, the black in her eyes fading into the green he loved. As Hannah returned to the forefront, tears swelled over her lids and streamed down her face. She rushed into his embrace, and Peter held her as if letting go would end both their lives.

"Peter," she managed to say between heaving sobs.

"I'm right here." His fingers combed through the auburn waves on the back of her head. "I'm so sorry this is happening to you."

"It hurts," she said. "This... this *thing* inside of me."

He pulled away from her and took her face in his hands, his palms warming her chilled pink cheeks. "I'm going to get you out of here."

The color and life left her face as quickly as it had returned. Her lips curved back into the insidious smile, and her eye color reverted back to black. "No," she said, her voice monotone and unfeeling. "You won't." Before Peter could process the change, she walked back to Troy and stood beside him.

"Where's the hunter, Kaylen?" Troy asked. "Is she battling it out with the others?"

His concern shifted from Hannah to Kaylen. "What do you want with her?"

"Come on, Peter. A demon contained inside a High Priestess, one who has a strong command of spells? With that kind of power, what *wouldn't* I want with her?"

"She's a hunter. Her whole purpose is to eradicate you."

"But, she would be an invaluable asset in locating portals."

"She wouldn't turn."

"Everyone turns. Don't you understand? The so-called 'dark side' is so much more favorable to you humans than trying to do good. You are all built with two purposes: selfishness and sin. Opening even one portal would be beneficial to your kind in every way, even for a hunter. Can you imagine if we opened them all? With you as our guide and Kaylen as our hunter to find the portals, it can all be a reality. Everything you've ever dreamed of can and will come to pass." He chuckled. "Even those things you keep hidden deep down where the slime grows. All you have to do is open one little door."

"You're going to kill Hannah anyway. It's required to open the portal. Sacrifice of Demon. Nothing you have to offer me will make me change my mind."

Troy shook his finger and stepped forward. "What if I told you there was a way to open the portal without killing Hannah?"

Peter froze, silent. Was it possible to save Hannah after all?

"She'd die, of course, but then I'd bring her right back."

"You... you can do that?" Peter asked. "Would she still be Hannah?"

Troy tilted his head from side to side. "Maybe with a few quirks, but nothing you two couldn't work through."

Peter recalled Kaylen's statement about the lies demons tell not always being too far from the truth. There had to be a catch with this offer to save Hannah. He had to stall long enough for Kaylen to come in and save them all.

"You can't count on her, you realize," Troy said. "The hunter can't help Hannah."

Eyes narrowed, his lips curving down, Peter stayed silent. He didn't want to say anything to infuriate the demon or risk further harm to Hannah. Still, curiosity at Troy's statement gripped his brain.

"You don't know, do you?" Troy sniggered and gripped Hannah's arm. "This here is just a shell for a demon. If the demon dies, so does she."

Peter's confusion wouldn't allow him to remain quiet. "But, you said you can bring her back."

"I can. The hunter can't."

"I don't understand."

As if sharing a secret, Troy leaned forward and whispered, "Exorcism kills the vessel."

Peter's heart understood the statement before his mind could process it. The thumping in his chest filled his ears.

"If the hunter walks through that door," Troy said, pointing to the barn entrance, "Hannah will die. Her only chance at survival is if you open the portal."

"That's not..." Peter shook his head. "No. That can't be

right." Kaylen would have told him if exorcism killed the vessel, wouldn't she?

As Peter reeled with the possibilities that Kaylen had withheld that information – something that affected the entire situation – Troy nudged Hannah and turned to her. "We're running out of time. Expedite this."

Hannah moved toward Peter, who instinctively stepped away from her. He soon ran out of space, as his back thudded against the barn wall. Before he could react, her hands reached around his throat and squeezed with a strength much greater than that of a human. His own hands flailed up, his fingers clawing at her, but she didn't release him. He tried to call her name, to beg for his life, but her grip refused him the ability to speak.

Within seconds, his feet lifted off the ground, and Peter's thoughts spiraled into a black oblivion. His eyelids fought against his attempts to keep them open, and his lungs burned with the fire of a thousand suns. An eternity passed as he stared into the eyes of the woman he had known his entire life, her own reflecting back a vacant evil that stilled his heartbeat.

His body dropped to the ground, but he remained floating inches above the ground. He lifted his hand to his chest, but his heart failed to beat. The weightlessness that carried him was unlike anything he had experienced while walking.

Am I dead?

A strange hue of orange overshadowed the rest of the barn, as if the sun were setting indoors. Something tugged on Peter, like earlier when he had walked, and he glided toward the back of the barn, toward the portal. It had changed from the time he first saw it – or maybe it appeared differently since he had entered his spirit form. A ghostly fog swirled orange and red, leading into a never-ending vortex.

Leading to hell.

But, it wasn't open. Yet.

Hovering over the portal, Peter marveled at the sudden rush of knowledge in his mind. He couldn't possibly know anything about the portal – Kaylen hadn't elaborated on any of it – yet it was all there. Everything he needed to know about the portal: its interdimensional existence, how it worked symbiotically with the world he knew, and how to crack it open to let the demons escape.

"Open the door, Peter."

Troy's voice behind him drove him to the brink of madness, but he refused to go over that cliff, the same one from which his mother had plummeted until it destroyed her and claimed her life. He saw it now, all of it. The things she knew, she *sensed*, and the gifts she couldn't control. She had once told him there was only so much the human mind could handle. She had been right.

"Save yourself," Troy said. "Save Hannah."

Peter's eyelids slid shut, and pain squeezed his heart until it exploded. If Kaylen came in, she would exorcise the demons and possibly kill Hannah. It might be possible that Hannah could survive the exorcism, possible that Troy had lied about that, but could he take that chance with her life?

And, then, he felt it. An unusual sensation of a binding, like a rope tied around his waist, tethering him to something unseen. A calm washed over him, as if he wasn't alone. As if Kaylen stood next to him. Even closer than that, somehow.

The binding spell, he thought. He thought it was only there to keep him connected to her during his last walk so he could find his way back, but the emotion bubbling inside of him was far stronger than anything he might experience on his own. He understood what her demon had meant about the blood spell and the demon's surprise at her performing it. Their link was nearly unbreakable, and its power far surpassed any normal bond.

In his spirit's eye, he could see her outside the barn standing over writhing bodies of his townsfolk, finishing up her exorcism spell. Her thoughts, emotions – everything – melded with his mind, and he suddenly comprehended her motivation for not telling him about exorcisms possibly killing the vessel. She worried his attachment to Hannah would prevent him from saving his town, from blocking countless demons from entering their world. Kaylen had a far greater purpose in this life than he had imagined, and it was now his purpose, too. One life couldn't stand in the way of her mission, and if the demons came into the world, Hannah would most likely still die, along with everyone else he ever cared about.

He whirled around and faced Troy, whose demon was now in full view. It appeared almost the same as Kaylen's demon, with slight changes in the structure of its head and features. Peter sensed its strength, which was much greater than Kaylen's demon, and though it terrified him at first, he refused to let fear swallow him. Through their bond, he drew on Kaylen's strength and stared down the demon.

"No." The word left his lips in a voice he didn't recognize, one that came from a place he couldn't see, but he felt. Every bit of anger inside of him over the state of his town, the possession of Hannah, and Troy holding Hannah's life hostage steadied his spirit.

The demon's eyes widened for a second before it snarled, an otherworldly ooze dripping from its decayed teeth. "Open the door, or I'll kill you all!"

Though its voice rattled through the barn, it failed to shake Peter's resolve. Kaylen's stride toward the front of the barn door flashed through his mind, and he grinned. "You can huff and puff all you want, little wolf, but the portal will never be opened."

The demon lunged at Peter.

"*Regna terrae, cantata Deo...*" Kaylen's voice boomed through the barn, an undercurrent of her true power in her tone.

Hay and dust kicked up as the demon collapsed. Its scream echoed in Peter's ears as the exorcism spell continued, but Peter was unfazed by it.

Satisfied that Kaylen had the demon under control, Peter moved around the tractor, to where he heard Hannah's cries for help. She had fallen near his body, and a pang of regret lanced his heart. He went to her and knelt beside her. As he watched her in the painful grip of death, he couldn't help but wonder if there was a way to still save her. Reaching for her hand, he held it the best he could in his spirit form.

At his touch, Hannah's spirit emerged from behind the demon's mask. Her pleading gaze locked with his, and, in that instant, he knew.

"Hannah," he said. "Come with me."

"I can't," she said. "It won't let me go."

"Fight it. Don't let it take you."

"It's too strong."

"No, it's not." He wrapped his other hand around hers and gripped it tight. "Not stronger than we are, together."

He barely tugged at her when he felt her release from her body. Her spirit rose from the ground and rushed to his. He embraced her, holding her head against his shoulder, neither of them speaking until he heard the last words of the exorcism spell.

Peeking over her shoulder, Peter watched fire consume the demon inside of Hannah's body until nothing remained except an acrid, black smoke. Once the smoke dissolved into the air, he broke away from her. "It's time to go back now."

"I don't know how."

"It's easy," he said. "Just let go."

He dropped her hand, and her spirit flew backward, down into her body. Her eyelids cracked open, and she rolled to her side, rubbing her eyes as if waking from a deep sleep. She pushed herself to her knees and quickly crawled to Peter's body. Tears leaked down her cheeks as she called his name.

The familiar feeling of being sucked back to his body gripped his abdomen, and he opened his eyes to see Hannah kneeling over him. "It's okay," he whispered. "I'm here."

She fell over him, her arms attempting a hug, her cheek landing on his chest. "I thought I killed you. I didn't mean to... didn't want to... I'm so sorry!"

"It wasn't you," he said. He kissed the top of her head. "But, I might need some help up."

She jumped off him. "Oh my... I didn't realize... Are you hurt?" She stood up and reached down for him.

He used her hand to pull himself to a sitting position, then got to his feet. "I'm fine," he said. "I'm more worried about you."

"What happened, Peter? There was something inside me... it made me... I almost killed you. And, Troy was... he was—"

"I'll explain everything," he said. "But, we have to find Kaylen first."

"Not if I find you first."

He whirled around at Kaylen's voice. She leaned against the tractor, gripping her side. He raced to her and put an arm around her. "Are you okay?"

"I'm good enough." She looked at Hannah, and a small smile claimed her lips. "You're alive."

Hannah nodded. "Thanks to Peter. You, too, I suppose, but I have no idea what—"

Kaylen stumbled forward, and Peter grabbed her arm to hold her up. "You're not okay," he said. "What can I do?"

"Get Hannah to the truck."

"What about you?"

"I still have to close the portal. Can't risk this happening again." She started walking again, with Peter's help, and stopped when she reached Hannah. Gripping Hannah's upper arms, Kaylen leaned over and whispered something to her.

When she straightened up again, Peter noticed the confused creases on Hannah's forehead.

"You understand?" Kaylen asked her.

Hannah nodded.

"Good. Don't you forget. No matter what, never forget. *Semper memento.*" Turning to Peter, Kaylen said, "Take her to the truck. I'll be out shortly."

Peter faltered. "But—"

"I'll be okay." Kaylen turned around and headed back to the portal.

Peter and Hannah exited the barn in silence, though he desperately wanted to ask what Kaylen had told her. They walked around the bodies of their fallen friends and made their way to the truck. He helped Hannah into the passenger side, then climbed into the driver's seat and started the ignition. He knew Hannah had questions, but he wasn't ready to answer them. *Maybe tomorrow*, he thought. Once he had a chance to sort through what had happened.

A bright flash of orange through the barn windows caught his attention. He leaned over the steering wheel and squinted, but couldn't see Kaylen. A rumble controlled the ground around them and rattled the truck. He held onto the steering wheel with one hand and onto Hannah with the other.

"Peter?" Hannah cried out. "What's happening?"

Before he could answer, the barn collapsed into rubble. A dust cloud rose from the debris, and Peter yelled at Hannah, "Stay here!"

He jumped out of the truck and ran toward the barn. "Kaylen!" When he reached what used to be the sliding doors, he shielded his mouth and nose with the neck of his shirt to help block out the dust. He climbed over some of the wood, but had difficulty seeing through the clouded night.

"Kaylen!" He stopped moving and listened for any sound.

Nothing.

"Kaylen!" He forged ahead, deeper into the center of the collapse, avoiding sharp edges of tools sticking out from the wood. She had to be there. "Come on, Kaylen."

He paused again, closed his eyes, and focused on their bond. It pulsed inside of him, providing him the proof of life he needed. Letting his senses guide him, he kept his eyes shut as he moved through the debris, to where the back of the barn had stood. His eyes opened. The tractor remained standing tall, and he shifted some wood out of the way and lowered himself to the ground. Relief filled his veins as he spotted her underneath the tractor.

He grabbed her arm and helped her out from her hiding spot. As she rose to her feet, he pulled her against him. "Don't you ever do that again," he said.

A small laugh escaped her. "I'll try."

He released her and wiped some of the dirt from her cheeks. Holding her face in his hand, he pressed his lips to hers and engaged her in a frantic, needy kiss. As much as he cared for Hannah, the bond between Kaylen and himself had taken over every part of him. He knew nothing else but his desire for her, one that had started on its own, but grew to unimaginable heights under the influence of the blood spell. Part of him knew, however, it would have reached that even without magic.

When they parted, Kaylen asked, "How's Hannah?"

"She's fine. Confused, but fine. I don't know how to explain any of this to her."

"I wouldn't worry about it right now," Kaylen said. "In fact, it's probably best if she sleeps on it for a night."

"I thought the same thing. What now?"

"Let's get her home safely. Then, I'm ready to sleep on it myself. Although, you still owe me an explanation of how you saved her."

"Just as soon as we get home. I promise." He took her hand and led her through the debris, far away from the closed portal.

Chapter Thirty-six

Peter startled awake. After he adjusted to the familiar surroundings of his bedroom, he rolled over. Patting the empty space next to him in the bed, he smiled at the memories of his time with Kaylen after they had returned home from closing the portal.

His palms dug into his eye sockets, rubbing away the remaining drowsiness. Glancing at his alarm clock, he realized he had grossly overslept, though he wasn't surprised. They hadn't climbed into bed until well after four in the morning, and it was much later than that when they had finally ceased sharing intimacies and drifted off to sleep.

He pulled on a clean pair of jeans and T-shirt and descended the stairs to find Kaylen. He peeked into the kitchen first, followed by the living room and the hall bathroom. Just as he was about to check the backyard, he heard the front door shut, sparking his curiosity. A lump in his chest moved into his throat and restricted his breathing.

Pulling open the front door, he spotted Kaylen with her hand on the door handle of a car, one he was certain she had stolen, a duffel bag of his slung over her shoulder. She paused when he called her name, as if determining if she should acknowledge his presence or continue with her escape.

His lips parted to speak her name again, but he stopped when she turned around. Her head slowly lifted until their eyes met, but she did not say a word. Her eyes said all he needed to know.

Not wanting to accuse, but not wanting to put ideas about leaving him in her mind, Peter avoided the topic. "It's a beautiful morning," he said, not wavering his gaze from her face.

A half-laugh escaped her, followed by a warm smile. "It sure is." As the smile left her lips, the air thickened between them. "Peter, I don't want to—"

"Then don't," he said. "Just come back inside."

"I don't have a choice."

"You always have a choice."

"I didn't want you to find me leaving. I knew how hard this would be, for the both of us."

He gestured to her bag. "Looks pretty easy for you."

"I promise you, it's not."

"Did I do something, or—"

"No," she said quickly. "You've not done anything wrong. If anything, you've done everything too right."

"Then I don't understand why." He closed the distance between them. "You don't have to leave."

"You don't want me to stay."

"Of course, I do. Why would you say that?"

"You don't," she whispered. "You know that me staying would be all kinds of complicated for you and me."

He tugged at the strands of dark hair hanging over her left shoulder. "I don't know that for sure. I can prove you wrong. Prove *us* wrong."

"It's too late, Peter."

"So, you were going to just leave me wondering where you had disappeared to?"

"No. There's a spell that will wipe your memory of me, wipe everything that you've been through. Something that will put your life back on its rightful path."

"A spell?" He shouldn't have been surprised, but the words knocked him back.

"It's the best way – the *only* way – to make everything that happened to your town right. Your town won't heal without it. You won't heal."

His mind crawled through the events of the past several days. "I don't understand how a spell to make us forget will explain all the deaths."

"My people are already on their way to handle the bodies at the barn. You won't even know they've come and gone. I don't know how your town will explain the deaths, but somehow, it always works out."

He flinched. "You've done this before? Did you know... Last night when we were... Did you know you were going to leave?"

"I'm so sorry, Peter."

A pain stronger than any heartache he had ever experienced shot through him. "But, we're bonded together. That blood spell you did—"

"You'll be fine," she said. "In a few minutes, the blood spell will have no hold on you and you won't remember me at all."

"I remember you right now." Out of desperation, he grasped her hands and pulled her to him. "There's nothing preventing you from... You don't have to do that spell."

Tears brimmed her eyes and threatened to spill over. She sniffed them back, and her voice cracked. "I already did the spell. It will take effect as soon as I cross the city line."

His hope drowned in a well of anticipated loss. "Then, you don't have leave at all. We'll keep you here, safe in town."

"I can't stay here forever. I have other jobs to do, Peter. Other people who need my help."

He knew that, knew it more than he wanted to. He battled the urge to keep arguing for her to remain with him. There was no point. Instead, his fingers brushed through her hair, and he palmed the back of her head. She met his lips halfway and engaged him in a deep goodbye kiss. Her tears dampened his cheeks, and he did all he could to remain strong, to not show weakness or his desire for her to stay.

The kiss came to a reluctant close, and Peter's breathing hitched on his rapidly beating heart. He released her, and she granted him one last smile before moving to the car. The engine turned over, and he watched Kaylen drive away, waiting until her car disappeared until he let go of his own tears.

Epilogue

Three years later...

The oak trees covering the rolling hill provided Kaylen with the perfect vantage point to keep watch. She dug in her backpack and retrieved her binoculars. Focusing the lenses, she caught sight of the toddler running across the playground. His mouth open in a toothy smile, his sandy-brown hair parted by the wind, the child bounded through the sand without a worry for the evils in the world.

Kaylen had to smile at the image, but her mood dropped as her gaze followed the boy to his parents. He leaped up in Sheriff Peter Holbrook's arms, and Peter swung him around in several circles. Next to him, Peter's wife, Hannah, laughed. Her hands clasped underneath her pregnant belly. Eight months along, if Kaylen remembered correctly – which she did.

Leaving Peter and the town of Nowhere had not been easy. Though she had been quickly erased in Peter's mind, along with any sign of the blood spell binding them together, she had not been so lucky. Day after day, month after month, the binding had slowly dissolved, but even three years after she left him, she still felt his presence. Still longed for him.

Every so often, she checked up on him, though always at a distance, with others relaying back his status to her. This had been her first trip back to Nowhere to see him in person. She had no intention of revealing herself to him, or to anyone in the town. She had doubted her motives when she first felt the desire to drive there, but she followed her instinct, hoping it would help her finally get over him.

The words she whispered in Hannah's ear the night she closed the portal echoed through her mind. *Give Peter a chance. You both deserve it.* The suggestion seemed to have taken root in Hannah's mind, and Kaylen's simple spell to never forget kept it there long after all other events had been forgotten.

It hadn't taken but a week after she left for Hannah and Peter to start dating. A few months later, they became engaged, and they married shortly thereafter. Now, they had a healthy two-year-old son with a daughter on the way. Living their perfect lives in small-town America.

You still love him. You won't ever stop loving him.

The sound of her demon's voice resounding through her mind startled her, but only for a moment. "I never loved him," she whispered to it. "It was infatuation."

You fell in love with him before you met him. Studying his files, night after lonely night. The handsome sheriff and the lost, little witch. You wanted him to save you from this life. From yourself.

"You don't know what you're talking about."

I know your every thought. You can't lie to me.

"No, but I can ignore you."

Not forever.

Her cell phone vibrated in her jeans, disrupting her attempt at healing her still-aching heart. She pulled it out of her pocket and groaned when she saw Shane Wallace's name written across the screen.

"Yeah?" she answered, letting her tone reflect her displeasure at his interruption.

"Where are you?"

"Nowhere, really."

"Well, wherever you are, come back in."

"I'm on my very short vacation, remember? Besides, I don't really feel like taking on a case right—"

"We have a lead on the grimoire."

His words stopped her from further argument. The grimoire – the ancient spell book that could possibly contain the spell to rid her of her demon – was never far from her mind. After all, if she didn't have a demon living inside of her, she might have been able to make a life with Peter, or someone like him.

"Where is it?" she asked.

"It's just a lead, but sources are pointing me toward Virginia."

She huffed. "I just returned from the East Coast."

"I take it you don't want to be demon-free like the rest of us."

She put her binoculars back in her bag. "Fine. Send me the coordinates?"

"Actually, you need to come back here first."

She slung her backpack over her shoulder. "It'll take me about four days to get there," she said, knowing it wouldn't take half that amount of time.

"Make it two." Shane disconnected the call.

She shook her head and shoved her phone back in her pocket. Looking toward Peter, she drew a deep breath and let the pain of losing him wash over her one more time. She had to start moving forward with her life if she ever planned on fully erasing the bond between them. Finding the grimoire was the perfect start.

She forced a smile as she stared at the perfect growing family. There was nothing more for her to think about. Even without the binoculars, she could see the serenity hovering over Peter and Hannah. Given her life and demon-filled baggage, he was happier than Kaylen could have ever made him. He would live out his life with Hannah and his kids and never remember a time when demons almost destroyed his town.

Exactly the way it was always meant to be.

###

More by Angie Martin

The Boys Club

Winner ~ Silver Medal for Suspense Fiction in the 2014 Reader's Favorite International Book Awards

Growing up a homeless juvenile delinquent left its mark on Gabriel Logan. He lived a throwaway existence until a former FBI agent recruited him for a fringe organization for boys like him, ones who could operate outside the law for the sake of justice. As an adult, he sets an example for the others and is slated to take over their group, until his work results in the murder of his pregnant wife.

Going through the motions of everyday life, Logan does only what's required of him with one goal in mind: kill Hugh Langston, the man responsible for his wife's death. When he's handed the opportunity to bring Langston down, he jumps at the chance, but the job will challenge him more than anything in the past. Not only does he have to save Langston's daughter from her father's hit list, but the job seems to have come to them a little too easily. Logan must find a way to not only rescue the one woman who can take down his biggest enemy, but also look into the men he trusts most to discover which one of them is betraying The Boys Club.

Conduit

Bestseller on Amazon US and Amazon UK
Winner ~ Gold Medal for Paranormal Fiction in the 2014 Reader's Favorite International Book Awards

How do you hide from a killer when he's in your mind?

Emily Monroe conceals her psychic gift from the world, but her abilities are much too strong to keep hidden from an equally gifted killer. A savvy private investigator, she discreetly uses her psychic prowess to solve cases. When the police ask her to assist on a new case, she soon learns the killer they seek is not only psychic, but is targeting her.

The killer wants more than to invade her mind; he wants her. Believing they are destined for each other, he uses his victims as conduits to communicate with her, and she hears their screams while they are tortured. She opens her mind to help the victims, but it gives him a portal that he uses to lure her to him. With the killer taking over her mind, she must somehow stop him before she becomes his next victim.

False Security

Rachel Thomas longs for normalcy, but if she stops running, she could die…or worse. Chased by a past that wishes to imprison her, haunted by dreams that seek to destroy her, Rachel finds solace in a love she could not predict. A love she cannot deter.

Mark Jacobson is the man who never needed love. He has his bookstore, his bachelorhood, and his freedom. In the moment he meets Rachel, he is swept into a world he didn't know existed. One filled with the purest of love. One filled with betrayal, lies, and murder.

Now Rachel and Mark are forced to face her past. The truth may kill them both.

False Hope

Rachel Thomas has spent the last four years running from her past. Forced into Witness Protection and exiled from the rest of the world, she manages to survive, but still lives each day in fear of being found again while trying to overcome her emotional wounds and past misdeeds as a criminal.

Mark Jacobson wants nothing more than to provide Rachel with the normal life she's always wanted. Dealing with his own scars and helpless to change their situation, he struggles to maintain his tenuous hold on his anger.

To find peace in a world she can share with Mark, Rachel agrees to help the FBI bring down all those who are after her. While the FBI believes she and Mark are safe, they are being watched closer than ever before. And, someone is ready to bring her home for good.

Shadows

From the bestselling, award-winning author of "Conduit" and "The Boys Club" comes a collection of short stories designed to illicit chills and keep you up at night. Shadows takes readers on a thrill ride through tales of hospital rooms and haunted houses, introducing everything from serial killers to the boogeyman. Includes "The First Step" written with bestselling author Marisa Oldham.

the three o'clock in the morning sessions

"the three o'clock in the morning sessions" is a poetry collection of works written over the span of almost fifteen years. This book also contains two short stories, "the door" and "brief love". All of the works deal with lost love or unrequited loves.

About Angie Martin

Angie is an award-winning, lifelong writer and firmly believes that words flow through her veins. She lives in Calimesa, California with her husband, two cats, and beloved dog. She also has two sons paving their own way in the world. She grew up in Wichita, Kansas and has lived all over the United States. Her work reflects her background in criminal justice and her love of Midwest life.

She has released several novels in the suspense/thriller, horror, and supernatural/paranormal thriller genres. She also has a poetry/short story collection ("the three o'clock in the morning sessions") and has contributed short stories to anthologies.

"Conduit" won the Gold Medal for Paranormal Fiction in the 2014 Readers' Favorite International Book Awards. "The Boys Club" won the Silver Medal for Suspense Fiction in the 2015 Readers' Favorite International Book Awards. It was also voted as one of the 2014-15 Top 50 Self-Published Books Worth Reading (ReadFree.ly). All of her works have won additional readers' choice and blog choice awards.

Website: http://www.angiemartinbooks.com

Fan Group: http://www.facebook.com/groups/angiesconduits

Facebook: http://www.facebook.com/authorangiemartin

Twitter: http://www.twitter.com/zmbchica

Angie's books: bit.ly/thrillingbooks

One Last Thing...

Thanks for reading! If you enjoyed this book, I'd be very grateful if you would post a short review on Amazon and/or Goodreads. Your support really does make a difference and I read all the reviews personally so I can get your feedback. Thank you again for your support!

Made in the USA
Columbia, SC
24 February 2020

88269021R00117